Love Set
IN
STONE

LOVE SET IN STONE

Staci Troilo

AIW Press, LLC
Lower Burrell, Pennsylvania
aiwpress.com

All characters and events in this book are fictitious. Any similarity to real
persons, living or dead, is entirely coincidental, and not intended by the
author.

ISBN-13: 978-1-944938-11-6

For Krista

You know the honor and horrors of military service.
You also know, because of PTSD, that it feels like you came home
with a monster inside you.
But know we only see the hero, the protector, the beauty.
So stretch your wings and fly. Soar. Be free.
And always know I love you.

Inspired by the poem
"God Bless the Gargoyles"
by
Dav Pilkey

One

Damien stepped off his plinth, his stone claws scraping off the ashlar before his feet thudded on the roof. He extended his arms above his head and his wings out to the side, the stretch doing nothing to work out the kinks from a full day of motionlessness.

With a low rumble, his body began its painful transformation from granite to flesh. He dropped to a crouch, the morphing and distorting of his rigid stone body into muscle and bone a nearly unbearable agony. When the change was complete, he sighed, wiped the sweat from his brow, and stood. This time when he stretched, his body found relief from the cricks and cramps of the sedentary hours he'd just passed as a gargoyle sentinel.

Now that the sun had dipped beneath the horizon, he was free.

At least until dawn, when the whole blasted thing began again.

Anael materialized beside him and ducked under Damien's right arm and wing. "Good morning. Or evening. Night? I'm never quite sure what greeting is appropriate for you."

Damien yawned, stretched again, and scratched the horns on his head. "Doesn't matter what time of day it is. None of it's good."

"I suppose I shall stick with 'hello' then."

"Why do you come here every day?" Damien asked. "What do you want from me?"

"I come because I'm your guardian angel. I want you to remember who you are, to act like yourself again."

Damien looked down at his grotesque body and sighed. He remembered all too well who he was. Who he had once been. He'd been trying to forget. Tried for centuries, to no avail.

"I'm here to help you." Anael grasped Damien's shoulder and stared into his eyes. "To remind you."

Damien shrugged him off and turned away. He looked at the city stretched out below him. "You want to help me? Break this curse and let me move on."

"God doesn't deal in curses."

"So who'd I make this deal with? The devil? That sure as hell doesn't bode well for me."

Anael bowed his head and made the sign of the cross. "Blasphemy will hardly help your cause."

"How could it hurt? I've lost track of the time I've spent here. Nothing ever changes. I'll be stuck here—stuck like this—forever."

Anael walked across the flat part of the roof and stood beside him. "No, my friend. Not forever. Only until you are true to yourself, to who you are. Only until you finally decide to live again."

"I don't want to live. Not like this!" He roared, and a few bats fluttered out from underneath a parapet. He took a deep breath and lowered his voice. "Look, it's been... honestly, I don't know how long it's been."

"The Normandy Campaigns in 1203."

Damien sighed. "Do you see what I mean? Look at me. Time has not been kind. I'm ready to move on."

"Physically, you look no different than when God brought you into this state of being. It's internally that you've changed. And you're right. The years have not been kind in that regard."

"Are you daft?" Damien turned around, leaned against the parapet, and stared at Anael. "You stand there with your ivory wings tucked inside your pristine green tunic. Those golden locks of yours glow even without sunlight. What do you know of haggard appearances?"

"I know you look the same to me."

"Look the same? I have pigeon shit on my horns! Hell, the fact that I even have horns is a nightmare. You want me to remember? You want me to live? Make me look like myself again. Maybe if I had a shred of humanity left, I'd feel more human. I'm nothing more than a fucking monster." He hung his head, all the fight in him drained away.

"Damien." Anael turned his charge to face the city. "Look around. What do you see?"

"A city."

"Stop being petulant. What do you see?"

Damien sighed. "I see a city."

Anael pursed his lips and glared at him.

"Fine. I see grime. Streets. Buildings. Lights in windows."

"You missed the most important part."

"Pray, tell."

Anael put his hand on the back of Damien's head and pushed it down. "What is directly below you?"

"A sidewalk."

"And on the sidewalk?"

Damien closed his eyes. He was so tired of this game. "I don't know. Gum? Litter?"

Anael huffed and released Damien. "Honestly, you're enough to drive an angel to curse."

"What do you want me to say?"

"I want you to say you see the *people*."

Damien looked down again. He'd grown to tune the people out. What with their constant yelling and horn honking and music blaring—if that noise could even be called music.

"Fine. I see people. Now can I be released from this curse?"

"I told you. It's not a curse. And when you're released is entirely up to you. It always has been."

Damien growled at him and flew away.

⚜

Damien beat his wings furiously, knowing his motivation was more from rage than from speed. He had no hope of getting away from Anael because if the angel wanted to, he could easily glide alongside him even at Damien's maximum speed.

Thank God the angel decided to leave him alone. Damien flew high into the darkness and soared in solitary isolation for miles. Even when his pace decreased, his anger did not.

Hot wasn't strong enough a word.

Incensed. Livid. Enraged. Inflamed.

Damn that angel, and damn that deal.

He needed to cool off. Dealing with Anael had become increasingly more frustrating.

Look around.

What do you see?

Let me help you.

The guy was a guardian angel, for Pete's sake. Surely he had more people to worry about than Damien's sorry ass. But there he was, every night, nagging him to death.

As if. Death would be a welcome change.

Decades ago, maybe centuries ago, Damien stopped believing there was any help for him. He wished he could just move on, fade away, cease to exist. Not existing at all had to be better than the living hell of his current existence. But Anael still believed. Anael still hadn't given up.

Maybe it was the angel's belief holding him hostage in his pitiful existence.

Damien flew under the clouds and looked down at the city of Pittsburgh stretched out below him. From his vantage point, he couldn't see the filth, the depravity, the misery. Couldn't see the people Anael pointed out, either. It was just a mottled expanse of pinpoints of light and pockets of darkness.

He dipped lower and scanned the city. A few miles north of him, the confluence of the Allegheny and Monongahela Rivers formed the Ohio River—the perfect place to cool off. He soared over Pittsburgh's mansions, universities, and corporate buildings straight to Point State Park. Nosing downward, he allowed his claws to trail through the fountain at the Point before plunging into the river.

He scrubbed at his head and neck to make sure he'd removed all the bird droppings, then he let himself float with the current.

Wonder what would happen if he stopped floating, just allowed himself to sink into the inky water and never surface. Would his lungs fill with water? Did he even have lungs? Would he die? Cease to exist? Perhaps this was the resolution he yearned for.

His mother had raised him to believe suicide was punished by eternal damnation. But he'd already died. Could he die again? Which death would God honor—his warrior death or his cowardly one?

Was it even right to call it cowardice? Didn't he need courage to take charge, make a change, end his misery?

Damien closed his eyes, exhaled, and felt the river envelop him, pulling him down into its watery depth. All he had to do was open his mouth, breathe in the water, and slip away. His lips parted.

He opened his eyes, saw a light, and smiled. So he'd made it. Heaven. Thank God. Relief washed over him, and he opened his arms, ready to move on.

The light advanced on him, engulfed him in warmth. All he saw was the blinding illumination—perhaps the Glory of God Himself.

But when the light dimmed, he wasn't in Heaven. He was back on the Godforsaken roof of Nathaniel Burton Mansion.

Anael glared at him, his amber eyes turning a fathomless black, his copper brows diagonal downward slashes on his forehead.

"I have to say," Damien said, "this is the first time in centuries I've seen you look less than beatific."

"Damn it, Damien!" The angel's voice echoed through the night.

"I guess I really did drive an angel to curse."

"This. Isn't. Funny!" If his last statement echoed through the city, this one reverberated to Heaven itself. "What were you thinking?"

"I told you. I'm done with this. It needs to stop. And if you won't stop it, I'm going to."

"And when eternity is worse than this?"

"I hardly see how that's possible."

The angel growled then uttered something in a language Damien didn't understand.

"What was that?"

"Enochian. Angel language."

"No, I mean, what did it mean?"

"Never you mind."

Anael grasped Damien's arm. He couldn't say what happened. It was as though the angel splintered him into atoms and scattered each one to the farthest reaches of the universe. Just as suddenly, his body slammed back together and he teetered on the edge of an abyss. Anael grabbed his arm to steady him. Below swirled a whirlpool of fire, shadows undulating in the flames. The smell of sulfur and brimstone wafted up the sooty black walls of the crag he balanced on, choking him where he stood. The cackling of demonic laughter overcame inhuman wails of agony, both of which echoed through the endless cavern.

Bodies. Those shadows were bodies, being sucked into the vortex and sent God knew where.

"God isn't the only one who knows," Anael said.

Damien jumped. "You—you read my mind?"

"I *always* read your thoughts. How else would I have known about your idiotic stunt?"

Damien decided to test the angel's abilities. He tried to block him out while thinking about where they were.

"You know damn well where you are. Stop trying to block me. It won't work. And stop testing me. It's a waste of time. I've never lied to you."

"You never told me you poked around in my head."

"You never asked."

Damien ducked as a black form sailed past him and landed with a violent explosion in the fiery river below. He lost his balance, and Anael steadied him again.

"Thanks," Damien said. "So, this is hell?"

Anael shook his head. "No. This is the entrance to hell. Once you pass through the vortex, you reach the first level."

"First level?"

"That's right."

"How many levels?"

The angel glared at him again.

"How long does it take to go through the whirlpool?"

"Longer than you've been a gargoyle."

Damien peered over the edge. The black mass that had plunged into the fire hadn't made any progress at all. It just seemed to be tossed about—fiery wave to fiery wave, sucked under and thrown back up—but never actually moving toward the center.

"Why did you bring me here?"

Anael sighed and shook his head. "Surely you don't need access to *my* thoughts to know why."

"To discourage me from trying to kill myself again."

The angel grasped Damien's arm and extended his majestic ivory wings. Damien was engulfed in a warm, bright light. Then he splintered into nothing, the shrieks of the damned ringing in his ears.

Damien came back together on the roof of the mansion. He patted the horns on his head, the wings on his back. Checked the claws on his toes and the tip of his tail. Solid. Corporeal. And all in one piece.

One grotesque, eternal piece.

Anael's eyes were back to their luminescent amber, and the severity of his countenance had also returned to its typical otherworldly beauty.

"So, that was... educational."

"Damien, you forget I've read your thoughts. I know more about what you think than you admit. More, perhaps, than you are even able to acknowledge with any truth or cognizance."

"Your point?"

"You don't want to die. And you certainly don't want eternal damnation."

Damien sighed. "No kidding. Who would? Doesn't mean I like things the way they are."

"Then change them."

"Don't you think I want to? What have I been saying to you for eons? I'm tired, Anael. I want to move on."

"Then embrace your destiny."

Damien roared again. "How?"

"I'm your guardian angel. I'm allowed to nudge you. I'm not allowed to give you a road map."

"Fine. *Nudge* me. At least get me started in the right direction."

Anael closed his eyes and mumbled something unintelligible.

Damien swore the angel counted to ten, but as he didn't speak Enochian, he couldn't be sure.

"Damien, come here."

He joined the angel at the parapet.

"Let's try this again. Look down."

He looked down, this time focusing on the people. They hardly interested him. At this time of night, usually the only people out were drunken revelers, prostitutes and their marks, and criminals.

"I'm looking down, Anael. I see the people."

"But what do you *see*?"

He'd punch the guy right in his chiseled jaw, but he knew it would only end up hurting his hand. "People. Just people. What the hell am I supposed to see?"

Anael disappeared.

Damien didn't care. Let the angel be angry and frustrated. He was angry and frustrated, too.

He punched the top of the parapet, scratching his knuckles on the stone and causing them to bleed. He shook his hand then sucked on the abrasion. While he stood there, he again looked down.

Nathaniel Burton Mansion was built on Fifth Avenue during the Industrial Revolution. Damien knew this because he had been removed from a cathedral in France, shipped to Pittsburgh, and mounted on a plinth on the roof of the robber baron's home. There he stood sentry for decades, lamenting both the loss of his beloved Europe and the immoralities of the American people. Over the years, he came to believe that it wasn't just Americans, but rather all people, who had been corrupted by technological advancements, the pursuit of money, or whatever had ruined modern society.

He'd lived in an era of honor. Now he existed in the time of greed and avarice.

So, he tuned the world out.

If Anael was right, it was time to tune back in. Damien refocused on the sidewalk below and saw the usual suspects. A woman of the oldest profession. A drug dealer or two. Inebriated pedestrians weaving their ways home or flagging down cabs. Nothing more than what he expected.

What caught his attention, though, were two scantily-clad women who looked out of place among the other people out at that late hour. They stood out of the glow of the street lamps, perhaps to avoid unwanted attention from the ruffians on the street. One was a voluptuous brunette, the other a slim blonde.

The blonde intrigued him. He needed a closer look.

Sticking to the shadows, he glided down to the sidewalk then crept closer to them.

She was stunning. Golden curls cascaded down her back. Fair skin looked almost luminescent in the moonlight. Slender, with high cheekbones and a petite frame.

The world fell away. She was the only thing he could see.

And she captivated him.

She coughed and waved at a cloud of smoke. And he began to pay attention to his surroundings. *Her* surroundings.

"I'm sorry," the brunette said. "I really thought I'd kicked the habit this time."

"Kind of hard to kick the habit if you step outside intending to smoke."

"Tomorrow. I'll quit tomorrow. I'll stop on the way to the library and buy patches or gum or something."

"Sure you will."

The brunette put her cigarette in her mouth and took

both of the blonde's hands in hers. "Rina. I promise. I swear on my sister's grave, I'll quit tomorrow."

Rina. Interesting name.

"You don't have a sister."

"I have you," the brunette said.

"Well, don't swear on my grave!" Rina yanked her hand away. She coughed at another puff of smoke.

The brunette stepped back and took the cigarette out of her mouth. Tipping her head up, blew three perfect smoke rings into the air above her before exhaling the rest through her nose.

"That's really gross, Gretchen."

"If you think that's bad, check this out." Gretchen took another drag on her cigarette, then she parted her lips. Smoke drifted out of her mouth, and she inhaled it through her nose.

"God, stop." Rina looked away.

"It's called a French inhale. Cool, right? Guys love shit like that."

"No. Not at all. I think when guys talk about tricks you can do with your mouth, they have something else in mind."

Gretchen swatted at her. "Naughty thoughts. Who'd have thought you had it in you?"

"I didn't say I did those things. I just happen to know what they are."

Gretchen laughed and inhaled again. "How do you know what they are if you don't do them?"

This time, Rina was the one doing the slapping. "Shut up. I don't do wicked things with my mouth."

Her friend laughed. "You think this was bad? You should see what I can do with a cherry stem and my tongue."

"Just stop." Rina looked at her watch, then she scanned the street. "Come on. You said a short walk, but we came at least two blocks. We need to get back."

Gretchen tossed the cigarette to the ground, ground it out with her toe, then linked her arm through Rina's. "Let's go."

Rina pulled away. "I'm not breathing this in the whole way back." She rooted through her purse, retrieved a bottle, then doused her friend in a scented mist.

Gretchen coughed and waved her hands to dissipate the cloud of perfume. "You're choking me."

"Don't even try that. If I can tolerate your cigarette smoke, you can tolerate a little body spray." She spritzed herself before returning the bottle to her bag.

"Come on." Gretchen slipped her arm through Rina's again as they headed down the street.

Damien inhaled. With his enhanced senses, he could make out the scent from the shadows where he watched them. The perfume smelled like springtime, fresh and floral. It suited her perfectly.

One last whiff, then he flew to a rooftop to looked down on the women. They headed toward a seedier part of town. His Rina didn't belong there.

Whoa. His Rina?

He didn't know where that thought came from. She wasn't his. Could never be his. He clenched his teeth and flared his nostrils. If he were a dragon, he would have shot fire into the sky.

What was worse? The miserable centuries he'd spent alone, or the knowledge that now he didn't *want* to be alone but would be anyway.

Again, he studied the women. They were two blocks away and turning into a building. He flew along the rooftops until he caught up to them, landing across the street from the establishment they'd entered. The sign above the door they'd walked through identified the place as Bar Belles.

The name was innocent enough. Brought to mind athletes and gym equipment.

Or fair maidens with demure personalities and chaste, ruffled skirts.

It was anything but.

Bar Belles attracted the most immoral of men. Some who left their wives at home with their babies while they spent their paychecks on booze and women. Others who would never marry because they lay with a different woman every night. Worst of all, those who detested women, who treated them like objects to be used for their own gratification and then tossed aside. If they were lucky.

More than once, Damien's miserable existence had been interrupted by commotion from this club. Fights that spilled onto the street. Gun shots. The cries of women being violated in the back alley.

Those disturbances happened at least once a week, maybe more, and the racket was so loud it traveled the two blocks over and three stories up to Damien's plinth on the roof. He'd investigated enough times to know the place was bad news.

What in the world was his Rina doing there?

He crouched in the shadows, determined to find out.

Damien didn't know how long he waited. Bar patrons came and went, hardly any able to walk straight, let alone drive safely —and not nearly enough of them took cabs.

He waited some more.

Prostitutes started drifting to the corner of the street, many of them leaving with men coming out of Bar Belles.

Still, he waited.

He kept an eye on a drug dealer on the opposite corner, but a ruckus on the street distracted him. Two men fought over the favors of one of the streetwalkers, who settled the dispute by inviting them to have a three-way. To Damien's disgust, the men eagerly agreed.

Repulsed, he scanned the street again. The drug dealer had disappeared. The sign on the door of the bar had been turned off. A bouncer let a few women leave then stepped back inside.

Still no sign of Rina.

Finally, the bouncer exited, held the door for Rina and Gretchen then locked up. "Which way are you parked?" When Rina pointed, he said, "Me, too. Let's go."

Damien assessed the man. Tall, muscular. Darkish skin. Long, dark hair tied back out of his face. Strange geometric markings tattooed on his arms.

They walked about thirty yards when Gretchen stopped. "I forgot my purse."

The bouncer started walking back toward the bar, but Rina put her hand on his arm and stopped him.

"It's late, Gretch, and I just want to go home," Rina said. "Can't you leave it till tomorrow?"

"Not if I want to get into my apartment or stop at the drugstore tomorrow. My keys and wallet are in it."

"Come on." The bouncer started walking toward the bar again.

"Tiny, no," Gretchen said.

Tiny? The guy was probably six-foot-four and three hundred pounds of muscle.

"It's late. Charlie will already be asleep, and I know Emily is waiting up for you." She turned and hurried down toward the bar.

"Really, it's okay," Rina said. "No one's on the street. We'll be there and back probably before you even get to your car. Just go."

"I don't know. I'd really rather see you both to Gretchen's car."

"Look," Rina said. "She already almost back at work. And I'll be with her. It's fine. We'll only be a minute behind you. Go. And kiss that sweet little face for me."

"Whose? Emily's?"

"Charlie's!" She laughed. The sound was musical.

He laughed, too. "If you're sure."

"Go. Gretchen's already inside."

Tiny waved goodnight and continued walking away. Rina turned and headed down the street.

Damien scanned the perimeter. That drug dealer was back on the corner, leaning into an expensive black car with tinted windows. No one else was down there. Then Damien looked up the street. It was deserted. Something felt off, though.

He heard the car pull away and looked for the dealer. He was gone. Could have gone with the vehicle or just disappeared back into whatever hole he'd slithered out of.

Satisfied the street was safe, he watched Rina. She had a graceful walk. A slight bounce to her step, a soft smile on her face. What put it there? Was she thinking of a man?

What business was it of his, anyway?

A few minutes later, Rina reached the front door of the bar. When she found it locked, she knocked.

Gretchen had tried that, too. But no one had answered. That's when she had walked around back. Damien didn't really think anything of that when it happened. He'd been much more interested in Rina's conversation with Tiny than in what Gretchen had been doing.

But now, studying the concern on Rina's face, he started to worry. How long could it possibly take to go in a back door, get a purse, and leave?

A muffled scream caught his attention just as Rina turned her head toward the noise.

Damien thought about going to check on Gretchen, but he couldn't abandon Rina when danger was imminent.

His heart constricted, squeezed by sharp stone claws of dread, when Rina ran toward the cry.

Two

Fear choked Rina, squeezing her throat to the point that she couldn't breathe. Why had she let Gretchen go back to the bar alone?

And what was happening to her?

As quickly as fear gripped her, it was chased away by determined bravery. No way would she allow anyone to threaten her friend. Rina ran along the side of the building, picking her way past random debris and listening for Gretchen. When her vision adjusted to the shadows, she saw her friend—

Pinned against the wall.

A man in black clothing had wedged his body between her legs. One hand held a knife to Gretchen's throat while the other reached down to the hem of her skirt.

Gretchen's eyes were open so wide, Rina could see their whites, even in the darkness.

She charged the man, putting her shoulder down and plowing into him. He lost his balance and grabbed for her. Both of them fell about a yard from Gretchen.

"Run!" Rina yelled. "Find help!"

Relief washed over her when she heard the rapid click of heels disappearing toward the street. Gretchen would be okay.

She, however, might not be.

Adrenaline kicked up a notch, flooded her system. Rina fought to untangle herself from the man she'd knocked down and, once free, scrambled to her feet. Two steps down the alley, her hair was grasped from behind. Her head jerked painfully as her momentum abruptly stopped, then her body was yanked back against the attacker.

Her scalp screamed from the assault. She was lucky she remained on her feet.

The man dragged her deeper into the shadows then shoved her against the wall. The brick surface scraped her skin through her thin blouse. She raked her fingers over his cheek, just missing his eye. Skin collected under her nails, and hot, sticky blood began to flow over her knuckles.

"You bitch!" He reared back and grabbed his face.

She scrambled to get away, but he grasped her arm. Tugged. Slammed her against the wall again.

Vision blurred. Legs wobbled.

Must stay awake.

Blinked. Again. Focused on his face.

His bloody face.

Black eyes glittered. Mouth turned down. Sickening snarl.

Must remember. Commit to memory. For ID.

If she lived.

She bit back tears, but her lips trembled.

He laughed and pressed against her, grinding her back against the rough wall even as he forced her legs open and positioned himself between them. The guy reeked of sweat and smoke and stale liquor. She turned away from the rank odor, but he grabbed her by the chin and turned her head back toward him. Then he held the knife to her throat.

She stood, pinned and helpless, much the same as her friend had been moments earlier.

Rina prayed Gretchen would find help to rescue her before things progressed further.

His free hand popped the buttons of her blouse before he squeezed her breast. Squeezed it hard. She yelped, thrashed, struggled to break free of his grasp. Then he let her go, choosing to reach for the hem of her skirt. He bunched it up to her waist.

She grew still, the fight in her replaced with paralyzing dread.

The cold steel of his blade at her neck nicked her flesh, and she felt a trickle of warm blood drip down her throat.

"Thought you'd play the hero, huh? Where's all the fight now?" The man's fetid breath caused her to gag, caused the knife to press deeper into the wound he'd caused.

How much farther could it go before he killed her?

How much further would he go before she welcomed death to the alternative?

A tear slid down her cheek, and she blinked it away. She would not cry. Would not play the damsel in distress.

No, she wouldn't go down without a fight. Help would come. Soon. And if she couldn't get away, she could hold on long enough for Gretchen to return with Tiny, a cop —anyone.

His fingers, cold against her leg, trailed too high up her thigh. She refused to think about where they were headed, what he had planned.

Blind desperation filled her lungs. She opened her mouth to scream.

The knife dug deeper.

"Make a sound, and that's the last one you'll ever make."

She closed her mouth, bit her lip. His body against hers gave Rina no room to strike or kick. The knife at her throat prevented her from even a head butt.

When he grasped her panties and yanked them to the side, she whimpered, tried to swallow the cry that could get her killed. The sound of his zipper lowering palpably grated on her nerves, echoed through her mind.

Gretchen wouldn't be back in time. No help, no intervention.

All that awaited her was the vilest of violations.

He laughed. "Not so feisty now, are you, bitch? Doesn't matter. It'll be good for me, regardless."

She leaned into the knife a little harder, searching for the courage to end it before the assault and the shame and the pain. But she couldn't do it.

This time she didn't blink the tears away. Instead, she closed her eyes and prayed to at least tune it out, to make no memories she'd struggle to forget. To just live through the indignity and the offense and come out whole on the other side.

Then a scream pierced through the silence of the night.

Rina opened her eyes.

She hadn't uttered a sound. The scream was her attacker's.

Her gaze met his, and she barely registered his terror before he was yanked away from her.

What happened? Where did he go?

She looked up and down the walkway, but no one was there. All she saw was the glow of the streetlights to her right and the fence behind the bar to her left.

A breeze wafted past her, and her skin chilled. Realizing the state of her clothing, she straightened her skirt and pulled her blouse together.

The hair on the back of her neck stood on end, goosebumps broke out on her flesh.

Someone had clearly stopped her attacker, but that didn't mean she was safe. The attacker could come back.

Or worse, whoever had scared him off could come for her.

Holding her shirt closed, she hurried back to the relative safety of the lamp-lit street. A large man with close-cropped hair stood over a formless lump of dark, rumpled cloth. Peering at the lump more closely, she saw it was a man dressed in all black, slumped against the bar door. His head lulled to the side, long dark greasy hair curtaining his face.

The man standing over him grabbed the stringy hair and turned his head toward her. She noted his eyes were bruised and swelling, his nose was crooked, and his nostrils and a fat lip dripped blood.

"Do you know him?" His voice was deep, low. Gravelly. Kind of sexy.

She shook her head, intimidated by his size, stunned by her errant thoughts, intrigued by his willingness to help her, a total stranger in a bad part of town.

He started to pull his shirt over his head. Rina's heart pounded in her chest. She had nowhere to go. He blocked the street, and behind her was a dead end. Surely he wouldn't... Not under a street lamp in the middle of the city?

She turned her head right. Left.

No escape.

He finished stripping off his shirt then held it toward her, gestured for her to take it.

She blinked, mostly confused. And a little taken aback by the sculpted body of the man. The defined, sexy, enormous man.

"For your modesty, miss."

She looked down. Her hands still fisted the two edges of her blouse together, covering the important bits as best she could.

"Th—thank you." Rina took the shirt and turned toward the bar before slipping it on. It dwarfed her, the shoulders almost reaching her elbows and the hem hanging down to mid-thigh. Even the head-hole was huge, looking more like a scoop neck on her, stopping just shy of revealing too much cleavage.

"Rina!"

She turned and looked up the hill. Tiny ran toward her followed about half a block away by Gretchen. A few other people huddled together across the street, staring and whispering among themselves.

The guy on the ground groaned, and her savior bent down and punched him again, knocking him out cold.

Tiny reached her, assessed the two men by the door, then studied her. "Rina. You okay? What's going on?"

Gretchen caught up, huffing, then threw her arms around Rina, crushing her in a hug before stepping back. "I got to Tiny just before he pulled away. We ran the whole way back." Gretchen panted, wheezed. Finally, she bent over, resting her elbows on her knees. "I called 911. Cops should be here soon."

"Rina? Talk to us. What happened?" Tiny wasn't winded at all, and his gaze wasn't on her, but on the two men again.

"I'm okay, thanks. This gentleman saved me." Gentleman? The guy may have saved her life and her virtue, but he hardly looked gentle.

The man stood up straight and faced Tiny. Before Rina could help it, a gasp escaped her. He actually made Tiny look —tiny. Probably had two inches on him and maybe twenty pounds. She once again appreciated the expanse of his chest, the chiseled abs. Scars marred an otherwise flawless and impressive physique.

Tiny extended his hand. "James Galufati. I work security here."

The large man looked at Tiny's outstretched hand for a moment, then reached out and shook it.

"Friends call me Tiny. And you are?"

The man's gray eyes bored into Tiny's, seemed to look right into his heart and soul before he decided to speak. Must have trusted what he saw, because he said, "Friends call me Damien."

Damien. She loved that name. It sounded powerful. Sounded strong. Honorable... hot.

She couldn't help it. She wasn't blind. Or deaf. Or frigid. And he did save her, so she was bound to be impressed, right?

It certainly had nothing to do with all those muscles. With his handsome features. With those full, kissable lips.

Or with those misty gray eyes she wished would turn her way and travel over her body like a lover's caress.

Seriously, what was wrong with her? Two minutes ago she was almost sexually assaulted, and now her thoughts were as lascivious toward Damien as her attacker's were toward her.

Sirens cut into her reverie, and she looked up the street. Flashing blue and red lights rounded the corner, a police vehicle pulled up beside them in front of the bar, then two officers got out. The shorter of them said, "What's the trouble here?"

"My name is Katarina Whitman. This is my friend, Gretchen Kiebler. She was being attacked back there, behind the bar. I helped her get free, but the guy grabbed me. She ran for help, and while she was gone, this guy ripped my clothes and tried—" She closed her eyes, shuddered at the memory, then opened them and continued. "Anyway, he tried to assault me, but Damien—"

She turned to introduce Damien, but he was gone.

Rina looked longingly after Tiny as he walked away. The cops released him after about fifteen minutes. He was hesitant to leave them alone, but when Rina reminded him his wife and little baby waited at home, he finally agreed to go.

She and Gretchen weren't so lucky. Rina was tired of retelling her story after the second time, but the police kept asking them both to repeat their statements. By the time she lost count of how often she'd recounted the events of the night, she was ready to scream.

Still, the police weren't nearly ready to be done with her

and Gretchen. EMTs cleaned and bandaged the cut on Rina's neck while she was being questioned. The two of them spent an additional hour with the police, repeating their stories again and again. Greasy attacker guy—whose name she learned was Dylan Ramer—kept contradicting them, but the cops finally cuffed him and put him in the back of their patrol car before finishing taking their statements.

She got the sense that if Damien had stuck around, the questions to her would have ended a lot sooner.

Why did he leave so abruptly? Did he have a record? Maybe he was dangerous.

The cops might not have believed her at all, but she had his over-sized shirt to prove her statement true. Or at least prove Damien had been there.

Rina was glad they didn't seize it as evidence of some kind. Not only did she not want to go back to clutching her blouse closed, she wanted to keep the shirt. It made her feel safe. Like a security blanket to a child.

And it smelled divine.

They separated her and Gretchen, and they went over her story about a dozen more times. It got to the point that she zoned out and babbled details from rote memory. If they asked her something else, she didn't even notice.

Finally, an officer said, "I think you've had enough for one night. The detective might have more questions for you tomorrow."

Rina was too tired to even acknowledge that. He drove her home, and she didn't even manage to thank him.

Once safely locked inside her apartment, she undressed and showered, scrubbing her skin almost raw to get the feeling of Dylan Ramer's hands off her body. After she dried off and rebandaged the wound on her neck, she slipped Damien's shirt back on.

She padded barefoot through her apartment, making sure

all the doors and windows were securely locked. Then she made her way back to the bedroom.

Something moved outside on the fire escape landing. Was that a shadow? A man? Had the cops let Ramer out already? Had he escaped and come after her?

Rina turned off her light and waited—her phone in one hand and an iron candlestick in the other—until her eyes grew accustomed to the darkness. Her heart beat so hard, she feared it would break her ribs. But she tamped down her fear and crept to the window.

Grasping the candlestick tightly, she raised it over her head and pushed the curtain aside.

Seeing a person standing there brandishing a weapon, she screamed and swung her makeshift weapon.

⚜

Rina lay in bed, glaring at the plastic she'd taped over the window.

No one had been on her balcony. She'd panicked when she saw her reflection in the glass and struck out. Because no one was there, all she'd managed to do was break her window and cut her wrist.

Now she had a bandage on her arm that matched the one on her neck.

And a raging case of insomnia.

The attack kept popping into her mind, and she kept blocking it out, determined not to dwell on it. Instead, she conjured up an image of Damien.

Damien knocking out Dylan to defend her.

Damien stripping off his shirt for her.

Damien and all those muscles. Sigh. Swoon.

Had she even thanked him? Would she ever get a chance to?

Why had he gone? Where had he gone?

She glanced over at the window again. So foolish. So frightened.

So scared, in fact, that she'd used thin plastic wrap rather than sturdy cardboard to block the elements from her bedroom. Sure, an old box would have given her more protection from wind and rain and creepy-crawly insects, but she couldn't see through a box. She could see potential threats through plastic.

And as she looked through the sheer sheets of film at the warped impression of the night behind it, she swore she saw something large fly past the moon.

Probably a bat or an owl.

Time for hot milk and a blindfold.

Or maybe a sleeping pill and a secure hotel.

Rina made her way to the kitchen, poured herself a shot of brandy, downed it. She poured a second. Then a third.

That was better. Took the edge off.

Bottle in hand, she made her way to the sofa then snuggled into the cushions, wrapping Damien's shirt around her like a swaddle. Not quite ready to doze off, she flipped on the television. Nothing like a little late-night shopping to put her right out. Even if she had to watch it through burned out pixels on eighty percent of the screen.

Just her luck. It was a tech hour, and the item up for sale was a television.

"Bet that one doesn't have burned out pixels," she muttered before raising the bottle to her lips.

"Hell with it. I've had a rough day. I deserve to splurge." She called the toll-free number at the bottom of the screen, rattled off her credit card digits, and even bought the additional warranty. After thanking the operator, she hung up and flipped off the television.

"No point watching a picture that's a poor imitation of a Seurat." She laughed aloud at her joke. Pointillism. Seurat. Missing pixels.

She snorted. "That's pretty funny."

A quick glance outside sobered her, reminded her why she was drinking and splurging and curled up on her sofa watching late night shopping through constellations of white dots.

The bottle almost slipped through her fingers, so she put it on the coffee table.

Then she closed her eyes, refusing to look out the window. If something was out there, she didn't want to know.

Three

D amien's body had been through more that night
than it had been in centuries.

He was used to transforming from stone statue
to living, breathing gargoyle and back. But this time, he not
only changed from stone to animate form, he changed from
gargoyle to flesh-and-blood man, complete with clothing.
Then back to gargoyle again.

Each change hurt more than the last. Rigid stone melting
into tissue and bone. Monster morphing and snapping into
the frame of a man. Human muscles stretching into mutant
creature again.

When dawn came, the transformation back to cold, hard
stone would be agonizing.

But human. He'd changed into his *human* form.

Damien sighed. He hadn't been human since the beginning of the thirteenth century—since he fought with honor
for nobility who had no appreciation for their privilege or his
sacrifice. At the time, he thought protecting Normandy for
Arthur of Brittany was his duty, was of utmost importance.

Centuries later? He doubted it even mattered. Monarchies

and empires rose and fell, overtook and crumbled, thrived and imploded. Yet, through all that, the world moved on. It wasn't about the land, the rulers. It always came back to the people.

People. Humans.

Ashes to ashes, dust to dust.

People were born. They lived, they died. The world continued to move on.

All but him. He'd died on the battlefield in France, fighting for what he thought was a just and noble cause. Instead, it was for land, for power, for prestige. And the monarch he fought for? Long gone.

Ashes. Dust.

It had all been for nothing. Could he even call his quest noble? All those slain men, and for what? An eternity to earn his happiness?

An eternity to atone?

Damien shook his fist at the heavens. "Why? Why offer me the deal? And why not let me out of it?"

His voice echoed across the rooftops and into the beyond.

As expected, no answer came.

Then Anael appeared.

He'd rather have no answer at all.

"I'm so proud of you, Damien." The angel took "beaming" to a whole other level. His smile was blinding in its brilliance, and his whole visage glowed.

"Proud of me?"

"Well, yes." His face slackened, his brow furrowed. "Are you not pleased?"

"Pleased? Do you know what the hell just happened?"

The angel crossed his arms over his chest. "Of course I do. And don't swear at me."

"Don't swear at—Are you kidding me? That's your reply to... to this?" Damien flapped his wings and waved his arms around.

"I fail to understand your frustration."

Damien sighed and grabbed his horns. "I have horns!"

"I know. I can see them."

It took all his willpower not to head butt the angel right off the roof. He took a deep breath then released it in a long-suffering sigh. "Anael. I've been a gargoyle for centuries. Never a change. Stone by day, monster by night."

"Monster is such a derogatory term, don't you think?" Anael looked at his nails and buffed them on his tunic. "I mean, after all, you aren't bad or demonic. Gargoyles were invented to protect churches and castles."

"Gargoyles were invented to drain water away from the mortar holding buildings together."

"That's true. But technically, you're not a gargoyle. You're a grotesque. Granted, that's an antiquated term, so—"

"Call me what you will. It doesn't matter. These stone monsters were not protectors. People invented the *myth* of them being protective spirits, guardians of the buildings they perched on."

"And yet, historically, lore says gargoyles are good."

"What does that have to do with anything? It's a folktale!"

"I'm just pointing out you aren't a monster, despite your thoughts to the contrary."

Why? Why had he railed at the heavens and prayed for an answer? Infinite silence was better than this.

"Damien, I know what you're thinking. I just don't understand why."

"If you can read my damn mind, then you should know why."

"Only if you think of why. I have access to what's actively going through your mind. God alone knows what's in your heart. And don't swear at me."

Damien knew if he opened his mouth again, he wouldn't be able to control what came out of it. Silence was probably for the best, as nothing he said would be fit for the ears of an angel.

Instead, he thought about his situation, putting to words concerns he'd been unwilling or unable to give voice to since Normandy.

The angel tipped his head, almost as though they held an actual conversation. Damien grew increasingly frustrated as time ticked on, moving closer and closer to dawn and his impending stone imprisonment.

Right before he screamed in frustration, Anael spoke.

"Damien, you clearly don't remember all the terms of your arrangement."

"I died. I was told I could move on or return to earth as a protector until I was ready to live the rest of my life. Pretty clear cut. And guess what? I've been ready to live the rest of my life since I took the deal. No luck on that front, though. On any of it, really."

"Nonsense. You've been a protector for centuries."

He gritted his teeth and spoke staccato words. "Gargoyles. Are. Not. Real. Protectors."

"You used to watch out for people. Those first few decades, in France. You dispatched many a ruffian to help the innocent."

Damien could barely remember that. Why had he helped? Why had he stopped?

Why did he even care?

"I'm tired. Of everything. Just make it stop."

"I see there's no dissuading you regarding your purpose here. I suppose we'll just have to agree to disagree."

Damien felt the tingling in his body, the sensation starting in his heart and spreading to his extremities. He glanced at the sky. The blackness had turned the darkest violet. Time was short.

"Anael, you know what I'm after. I need to know. How did I become human today?"

The angel scoffed. "You've ignored me for centuries and now you want to listen?"

Damien climbed onto the plinth, assumed the position he'd be in for the course of the day. "Anael. Please?"

His heart grew cold. Icy sludge clogged his veins, flowed slowly toward the tips of his claws. Stiffness settled on his torso, a weighty boulder of rigidity.

Anael stretched his glowing ivory wings and smiled at him. "That's what I've been telling you since day one. You've always had the ability. You just needed the motivation. Now you found her."

Damien's jaw dropped. The sun cracked the edge of the horizon, and his body petrified into a stone gargoyle guarding Nathaniel Burton Mansion.

This time, however, the gargoyle sported an open maw, a grotesque distortion to the already fantastic monstrous form it usually portrayed to the public.

Since 1203, Damien had spent half of every day as a statue.

But he'd never spent a longer one.

The angel had flown away as soon as he dropped his bombshell, and he wasn't continuing the conversation through Damien's thoughts. That left Damien with two options—sleep or ponder.

Like sleeping was even an option.

He spent the day obsessed with Rina and what she might mean to him. She consumed every second of his daylight hours, except for the times he wished he could move and shoo the birds away. All too often they landed in his mouth, and he desired nothing more than to chomp his jaws closed, chew the little beasts up, then spit them to the four winds.

When a particularly annoying hawk took care of business on the tip of his tongue, he thought his rage would melt his stone prison. Instead, he looked forward to a good scrubbing in the river while swearing never again to leave his mouth open before the sun went down.

And then his thoughts drifted right back to Rina.

Katarina.

Katarina Whitman.

What a beautiful name. What a beautiful woman.

What luck that she was his destiny, his key to freedom.

Or would she become just a bigger curse?

He screamed in his head for Anael, but the angel remained elsewhere, unwilling or unable to come to him during the day.

When the sun dipped below the horizon and the familiar pains of morphing to life began, Damien's pulse raced.

He stepped off his plinth, stretched, and roared.

Time for a good scrubbing. And better answers.

Every nightfall since Damien had become a gargoyle, Anael had appeared with hope on his face as bright as his smile. And every nightfall, Damien had grown irritated with the angel's optimism and love. Hell, with his very existence at some point.

This night was the first he'd ever looked forward to the angel appearing.

So, of course, he didn't.

After a quick scrub in the river, he flew back to his roof and waited for Anael. He continued waiting for what felt like half the night—in reality it was probably no more than fifteen minutes. Still no angel. Damien stretched his wings and soared into the night sky, well above the city where he could blend into cloud cover. At the very least, he was far from any street-lights or buildings that might catch him in their illumination.

He couldn't afford to be seen by humans. Particularly by the one human who caught a glimpse of him the night before when he peered in her window.

It wasn't like he was a creepy voyeur or anything. He had just needed to be certain she'd arrived home safely. The last thing he had wanted to do was frighten her. A night later, he felt the same way.

Before he knew it, there he was, perched on the roof of the building across from her apartment, staring at a flap of plastic where her window used to be—before he'd startled her into shattering it the night before.

At least this time he was smart enough to keep his distance rather than landing on her fire escape.

"Damien."

He'd been focused so intently on Rina's window that he hadn't seen Anael appear. When the angel spoke, Damien jumped and slipped off the roof. After he'd fallen a few floors, recovered, and flown back to where the angel waited, he shoved him. "What the hell, Anael!"

Anael looked at his chest where Damien's hands had pushed against him. Then he looked back at Damien. "I'd thank you to keep your hands off me."

"Where were you? And why are you sneaking around, scaring me like that?"

"I do have other charges. I can't be with you all night and all day. And I wasn't sneaking. I was appearing. With panache." He twirled his hand in the air and took a deep bow.

Damien took a deep breath. "I needed you. I thought to you all day. And ever since I woke."

"You don't need me for inspiration any longer, Damien. You found your purpose. Now it's up to you to seize the opportunity."

"Purpose? Opportunity? I don't have a clue what's going on! I was human yesterday. Do you know what that means? How I did it? How I can do it again?"

Anael leaned back and crossed his feet in front of him. Like he was reclining, but without any furniture to rest on. He merely floated, legs outstretched, hands behind his head. "I have a while. Work through it."

If he thought he could push the guy over the edge of the building, he would. No point in wasting the energy, though. Damien rubbed his hands over his head, wincing when the horns scraped his palms. "Anael. I don't know what I'm supposed to work through. Something is happening to me, and I don't understand it."

The angel stood, buffed his nails on his tunic, then looked at Damien. "What did your agreement say? Do you remember?"

"Something about remaining a protector until I found my destiny."

"So...?"

"So? So what?"

"Your body changed yesterday, yes? You took human form?"

"Yes. That's what I'm asking you about."

Anael grasped Damien's shoulders, bent down, then met his gaze with an intense stare. "So that means you found your destiny. Go get it."

"Go get it? Get what?"

"The woman. Katarina."

"The wom—How am I supposed to do that? I don't even know how I managed to change. I certainly can't approach her like this." He flapped his hands at his body.

"Honestly, Damien. Do I have to spoon feed you? When you saw her, what happened?"

"She was being attacked. I saved her."

"How did you feel?"

"Feel?" He thought on that for a moment. How did that make him feel? "Scared for her. Enraged at the guy who attacked her. Protective."

"Your instincts kicked in. This is the first time anyone has

inspired an emotional reaction in you. Your body just natu-
rally responded to what you needed from it. Namely, you
needed to appear human so as not to frighten her, and that's
how your human form manifested."

"Is it sorcery? Am I magic?"

Anael laughed. "No, no magic. At least, not in the sense
you know it. It's more like a miracle. Part of the deal you made
when you died."

"I got transformative powers in the deal?" For the first
time in centuries, Damien felt a buoyancy, a lightness. A hope
radiating through him. "How did I not know that?"

"You have transformed every dawn and every dusk since
that day. How did you *not* know that?"

Damien raised an eyebrow.

Anael sighed. "You were given the tools you needed to
bring your deal to fruition. You've always had them, and
finally, you're using them." His gaze grew sharper. "Don't
mess up. You won't get a second chance."

Hope dimmed as fast as it bloomed. "What do you
mean?"

"Katarina is the one. The one for you, the one you've been
waiting hundreds of years for. And she's in danger. Grave
danger."

"From whom?"

"Just stay vigilant. You need to protect her, win her over.
It's time your deal ended. One way or another."

"Wait. One way or another? What are the ways?"

"You and she find your happily ever after."

Damien waited, but the angel didn't continue. So he
prompted him. "And if we don't?"

Anael frowned. "Let's not think about those options right
now, shall we?"

Damien started to protest, but the angel disappeared.

"Damn it." He started raise his fist to the heavens, but

thought better of it. Instead, he looked over at Katarina's apartment. He didn't know about a happily-ever-after for them, but he'd be damned if he let anyone hurt her. Then he thought through all the ramifications of that.

It stole his breath for a moment.

He could, literally, be damned if he failed.

Four

Rina hadn't slept well. At. All. She'd been convinced someone was outside her window and was going to come in and hurt her.

Which would really have been something, considering she lived on the fifth floor.

Still, she couldn't stop thinking about the fire escape landing outside her window. A motivated attacker could make it up there. With a little luck and a lot of effort, maybe without being seen by anyone.

The thought made her blood chill.

The alcohol hadn't helped. It had made her thoughts run wild. It had also turned a moderate buzz into a major hangover.

When dawn broke, she stumbled into the kitchen to make coffee. Would have mainlined it if she could have. Instead, she waited for the pot to perk and downed the first cup, black and scalding, as fast as a shot of whiskey. After the tears and sputtering subsided, she poured another cup, added cream, then padded barefoot into her bedroom to stare at the plastic covering the window.

"I'm going to have to come up with a sturdier alternative."

Who was she kidding? She definitely didn't have the money to repair the glass. And she doubted she would be able to board the broken window without destroying the casing around it. Besides, even though she feared what was outside, there was no way she'd be comfortable not having the option to see what wasn't—or was—there.

"Guess I'm going to the glass shop." Ramen noodles for the next month, then.

As the fog started lifting from her brain, she grew more aware of how much pain she was in. Her back felt raw. Her head hurt from more than the alcohol, aching where it had slammed against the wall. Her neck stung where—no, she wasn't going to think about that.

Aspirin might help. And a hot bath.

She downed three Excedrin tablets then climbed gingerly into the tub, immersing herself in steaming water and bubbles. When her fingers pruned and the temperature cooled, she stood, drained the tub, then showered. Bubble baths always relaxed her, but she hated feeling like she had soaked in washed-off filth.

After dressing and drinking two more cups of coffee, Rina considered taking a nap. She was still a little sore, a lot hungover, and worried about work. She'd never make it through the late shift if she didn't get some rest. So despite the four cups of caffeine, she curled up on the sofa. Snuggling under a blanket, she closed her eyes. Just before drifting off, her phone rang.

"Why?" She sighed and opened her eyes. Phone in hand, she frowned at the caller ID then swiped her finger over the screen. "For the love of God, Gretchen. I'm trying to sleep."

"Sleep? It's nearly noon."

"I didn't sleep last night. Funny how being attacked in a dark alley can keep you up."

"I'm sorry, Ri. I should have listened to you."

"Apology accepted. Now can I go?" She closed her eyes and barely managed to keep the phone by her ear.

"Sorry, but no."

Rina growled and muttered something unintelligible.

"The police called. They have more questions and want to see us at the station. In half an hour. Don't you ever check your messages?"

"More questions?" She opened her eyes and scowled at the ceiling. "Didn't they get every detail last night? At least four million times?"

"Apparently not."

"Can you pick me up?"

"Sorry," Gretchen said. "My car got towed. You believe that? The damn cops kept us last night for hours, only for me to find they towed my freaking car while I was with them."

Rina sighed and sat up. "We'll just have to talk to them about that at the meeting. Give me ten minutes, then I'll meet you at the corner. We can share a cab."

"If you hurry, we might catch the bus."

"If I hurry, I'm going to look like a zombie. I need to at least get concealer over the bags under my eyes."

"Shouldn't take that long."

"I'd be faster if I wasn't still on the phone."

Rina chuckled when Gretchen ended the call without even a goodbye.

I wasn't that Rina wanted to take a cab. They were generally smelly and always seemed to cost more than they should. Besides, she didn't have the money to spare for frivolities like a cab when the bus would do. Neither did Gretchen. But after the horrors she'd suffered the night before, she didn't feel comfortable sharing a ride with strangers. Any one of them could be a violent criminal, just waiting to follow her off the bus and drag her into a dark alley.

No, she didn't have the money to waste on a cab. Especially now that she had glass to replace. But she didn't have the courage to risk the bus. Peace of mind had to be worth something, right?

So, despite Gretchen's request to hurry, she dawdled, which thankfully caused them to miss the bus. It was pulling away as she stepped out of her building and headed to the corner.

"If we run, we might catch it at the next stop," Gretchen said.

Rina only arched her brow in response. She wouldn't be able to catch it if she sprinted. Her bronchially-challenged friend? Not a prayer in the world. Rooting in her bag, she dug out her phone to call a cab.

"You made us miss it. You could at least call ride share."

She pulled up the listing for the cab company then tapped their phone number.

Gretchen scowled and took a pack of cigarettes out of her purse.

Rina ended the call then held out her hand. "Gimme."

"What?" She put one in her mouth and grabbed her lighter.

Rina snatched the cigarette, threw it on the ground, then stomped on it.

"What the hell? What'd you do that for?"

"Oh, let me see." She started ticking items off on her fingers. "One, because you couldn't run a block last night without wheezing like an asthmatic. Two, because you're complaining about money but throw away hundreds of dollars a month on these nasty things. Three, because they're disgusting, and I have no interest in smelling like an ashtray today. Four, because you promised you'd quit. Today. And five, because you swore on my life. Remember, *sis*?"

"Yeah, but after last night—"

"After last night, you should be more aware of the value of your life. Now, I've covered this hand." She held up the hand she'd counted on, waggled her fingers, then made a fist. "Do we need to start on the other one? Or is this one convincing enough?" She waved her fist under her friend's nose.

Gretchen burst into laughter. "Is that supposed to be threatening? You? Punch anyone? Let alone your best friend? As if!"

"I could punch someone."

Gretchen continued laughing.

"What? I could." When her friend kept giggling, she dropped her hand. "I fought last night."

That sobered Gretchen up. "Oh, sweetie. I know you did." She draped her arm around Rina. "I'm sorry. It was my fault that even happened. You're right. I said I'd quit. No need for violence."

Rina flung Gretchen's arm off her.

"But, you know," Gretchen said, "maybe it wouldn't be a bad idea to take some self-defense classes."

The cab showed up. They clambered inside.

Rina told the driver where they were headed then turned toward Gretchen. "You're worried about cab fare, but you want to take lessons at a gym?"

"What's that about the fare?" the driver said over his shoulder.

"I've got it," Rina told him. "Don't worry. And don't take the long way around."

He muttered something but kept driving.

"It doesn't have to be at a swanky gym. Maybe the Y has something cheap."

"You get what you pay for."

"Hey," Gretchen said, "some of those programs are pretty darn good."

True, but if she was going to learn to defend herself—which wasn't a bad idea—she wanted a pro to teach her.

"If money's an issue, Ri, maybe Tiny could show us a few moves."

"I want more than a few moves. Besides, he's busy with the baby. I hate to ask him to give up any free time for us."

"The cops might have a suggestion," Gretchen said.

"Maybe." She let her voice trail off with her thoughts. If she had to have training, wouldn't it be wonderful to learn from Damien? Bet he could show her all sorts of things.

The driver snapped his fingers in front of her face while Gretchen nudged her. She looked out the window. They'd arrived at the police station. "Sorry."

He grumbled something unintelligible as she fished money from her wallet. Because he was so surly, she only gave him a small tip. She wouldn't have given him a tip at all, but she understood working for tips. Wouldn't be right to totally stiff him.

Apparently the token tip got her point across. The cab's tires squealed as he pulled away from the curb, and Gretchen flipped him off.

"Come on," Rina said. "Let's get this over with."

Inside, they spoke with the desk sergeant and were told to have a seat. Soon a detective opened the door and beckoned them to follow him. At his desk, he had them sit in chairs facing him.

"Thank you for coming," he said. "I'm Detective Urbani. I just have a few questions."

"That's what the officers said last night," Gretchen said.

"I'm sorry." Rina looked at the name plate on his desk. Detective Stephan Urbani. Not a uniformed officer, but a suit-wearing detective. An expensive suit, at that. A suit-wearing, scowling, not-to-be-screwed with detective. She was the victim, not a perpetrator. What was with the suspicion and disbelief? What could he possibly want?

"I'm confused. What happened to the officers we spoke to last night?"

"Those were the arresting officers. They've submitted their reports. But the investigation then goes to a detective. This landed on my desk last night. And there are some lose ends I'm trying to tie up."

Gretchen looked as confused as she felt. Rina shrugged. "Okay. What loose ends?"

"Well, I spoke to the man you accused of assaulting you."

"Accused? No ambiguity there. He did assault me. Right after he attacked my friend."

Gretchen nodded.

Detective Urbani sat back in his seat, staring at her. "No, there's definitely ambiguity. He tells quite the different story. Says you and your friends rolled him for his money."

"You've got to be kidding me," Gretchen said.

"What?" Rina's pulse quickened. Her headache raged a war on her skull. "Give me a break. You don't honestly believe that, do you?"

"It's not a matter of what I believe. What matters is what the *evidence* says. And it's not so cut and dried."

"No, what matters is the truth." Rina couldn't believe it. She'd been violated, attacked. Why was he accusing her? Why was this happening? She leaned forward, tipped up her head, then pointed to the bandage on her neck. "As for evidence, what about this? What about the lump on my head, the scrapes on my back, the random bruises I have on my body?"

He drummed his fingers on the arm of his chair. "All of that is easy enough to fabricate."

"What about Damien? Have you interviewed him?"

"Ah, yes. Damien. I read about him in your statement." He leafed through papers on his desk. "Damien who? Where does he live? How do you know him?"

"I don't know him. Or anything about him. I just met him that night. He was a Good Samaritan. He saved me."

"Kind of hard to interview a ghost. He's in the wind. Could be he has a record and wants to hide. Could also be that he was in on it."

"Come on," Gretchen said. "Ramer is a dealer. We're hard-working citizens."

He smiled at her, his expression hard. "Yeah, at Bar Belles. One of the many... *working girls* they employ. Is that what happened? Ramer not a good tipper in the private rooms?"

"If you weren't a cop, I'd slap you for a comment like that," Gretchen said.

Rina grasped her friend's hand and squeezed. "Stop."

"Ri, he thinks we're—"

She shook her head. "Detective. Did you follow up on anything we said in our report?"

"I followed up on all of it. That's one of the reasons you're here."

"Well, if you did your due diligence, you know we aren't dancers at Bar Belles. We're waitresses. I have no first-hand knowledge of what happens in those private rooms, and I don't care to. I show up, do my job, and go home. Gretchen, too. We aren't 'working girls,' like you suggest. And you should know that."

"If you're as innocent as you say, you wouldn't work at an establishment like that. No, I'm thinking you work there to find your marks—lowlifes you can steal from. People who won't go to the cops because they got their money illegally. Only this time, things got out of hand, and you needed a story for cover."

"We work there because it suits our schedules and the tips are good."

"Good tips? At a strip club? I don't think so. Not unless you're dancers, which you claim you aren't. And even then you'd have to be damn good to rake in a decent haul."

Rina made fists, dug her nails into her palms to keep from screaming at him. "We work there because we need night employment, which isn't as easy to find as you might think."

"I think above-board jobs would be easier to find during the day."

"And I think you didn't follow up on anything we told the police last night, because if you had, you'd know we're in school during the day."

He stared at them. She clenched her fists tighter, ignoring the bite of her nails in the tender flesh of her palms.

"For the record, no," Gretchen said, "our tips aren't as good as the dancers' are. But they're a damn sight better than any we'd get pouring coffee a diner. These guys get drunk, they get enamored, then they get generous. *Without* us compromising our morals."

He picked up a pen, twirled it through his fingers. "So you say. But the money can't be that good."

"We get by," Gretchen said.

"You get by. Well enough to drop money on unnecessary items? Or do you need an extra influx to support your spending habits?"

Rina's stomach soured. She had a feeling he was leading them toward his big reveal, and some niggling thought in the deep recesses of her brain warned her against it. What did he think he had on them? What wasn't she considering, remembering?

"What spending habits?" Gretchen asked.

"I've pulled your financials. You're both swimming in debt. Yet you," he looked at Gretchen, "squander hundreds of dollars a month at super-centers and liquor stores. Money a poor college girl simply doesn't have."

"Just cigarettes," she mumbled. "Besides, I've recently quit."

"And you." He looked at Rina. "For funds being so tight, you dropped a hefty sum just last night."

"What? I was at work. I didn't even buy dinner."

"Maybe not. But when you got home, you ordered a Sony flat screen. Hardly seems like something you could afford on your current wages. Or something a victim would do after an attack. You should have waited a while to spend your haul. It would have been less obvious."

The blood drained from Rina's face. That niggling thought broke free and smacked her right between the eyes. The late-night drunken shopping spree. What had she been thinking?

Oh, right. She'd been avoiding the thing that went bump in the night.

"How dare you? I'm assaulted and report the crime, and you dig through my life? That's just another violation."

"No, ma'am. It's not. It's my job. One *I* work hard at. When Ramer's attorney informed us of his side of the story, I got to work. From my side of the desk, things aren't so one-sided. I'm just trying to get to the bottom of it all."

Rage and indignation fueled her comments before practicality could rein her in. "Your side of the desk? You, who earns a cop's salary yet is dressed in a designer suit that probably costs more than my monthly rent? Now I get it. You're on the take. Probably on Ramer's payroll."

She panted, struggling to catch her breath. It was Gretchen's turn to shake her head and shush her.

"I don't believe there's any law against dressing well. But I certainly don't owe you an explanation."

"Your denial just proves I'm right. I want a different detective. Or you're just giving my attorney grounds to have this case thrown out in court."

"Interesting that you assume this is going to trial. And with you on the defense."

"How could it go any other way, with a dirty cop working against me?"

"I gave you one free insult. I won't stand for a second."

"But it's okay for you to insult us?"

"The difference is I'm doing my job. You, on the other hand? Let's just say your behavior is proving Ramer's case."

"My behav—" She jumped to her feet. "Where is he? Bring him out here. Take me back there. Whatever. I need to see him."

"You really want to set eyes on him?" Gretchen asked. "After what he did to you? To us?"

"No, of course not. But I'll be damned if I'm going to let him sully my reputation after everything else he's done. No. He's going to have to look me in the eye and accuse me to my face." She turned to the detective. "And you'll be eating your words when you see the lies written all over his. Where is he?"

Urbani sat back and stared at her. "It's not our policy to let one defendant confront another."

"So, we *are* defendants?"

"Potentially. For now, let's operate like you are. Until we get to the bottom of things. I told Ramer, and now I'm telling the two of you. Stay away from each other. We'll sort things out, and then the courts can handle it."

"The courts can—Wait. What?" Rina plopped back down in her seat. "You told him to avoid us?"

He nodded.

"That means he's not here."

"We didn't have enough to hold him. His lawyer sprung him last night."

Rina groped for Gretchen's hand, found and squeezed it.

Her attacker was free. Free to follow her. Free to violate her again.

Free to watch her through her broken window.

She shivered and stood on shaky legs. "I'm assuming we're free to go."

"You may leave the station, but not the city. We'll be seeing you soon." He stood then led them toward the exit.

Rina led Gretchen around other desks, chairs, and people in the room. At the door, she stopped and looked at him.

"What would it take for you to change your mind and believe us?"

"I haven't made my mind up yet, so there's nothing to change. But if you want to know what will round out the evidence, I want to talk with Damien whatever-his-name-is. I need to interview your Good Samaritan."

After they left the station, Rina had to once again plead with Gretchen to take a cab rather than the bus. They'd both forgotten to mention the towed vehicle, and after the debacle with Detective Urbani, it was unlikely he'd help Gretchen get her car back fee-free.

Gretchen agreed to a cab and placed the call. When it showed up, they clambered inside, but other than giving their destination, Rina didn't speak. Both seethed the whole way back. Gretchen kept trying to vent her anger, but Rina kept shushing her. Given how thoroughly Urbani had invaded her life, it wouldn't surprise her if he interviewed the driver after they got out.

When they stepped out of the cab at the corner where they had met that morning, Rina finally let her friend rant.

Gretchen verbally-vomited all over her.

"I can't believe the nerve of that guy. How dare he? Suspecting us of being the aggressors. As if you would ever run some kind of scam like that. And accusing us of wasteful spending. While he's sitting there in that gorgeous suit! Hell, his haircut probably cost more than my whole outfit. Thinks he's better than me just because he's rich and smart and handsome and educated. I'll show him. When I get my degree, I'm going to make oodles more than him and throw it in his face."

So that rant took a turn awfully fast. Rina started to let her mind wander, but Gretchen didn't even slow down.

"Fake injuries? If he knew the kind of person you are, he'd

know better than to even suggest something like that. Why, if Tiny had been there, I bet he—"

Rina let her continue to blow off steam, but she completely tuned her out. She felt the same way Gretchen did —at least about their situation, if not the detective himself— but what would be the point of yelling about it? Wouldn't get them out of trouble.

And they were in trouble. Big trouble. If she understood correctly, they could end up in prison. Prison! Bad enough she'd been careless with her budget and shopped for frivolous things in the middle of a drunken panic-fest. Now she'd gone and provided Ramer's lawyer with, at best, reasonable doubt to clear him, and at worst, a motive for her robbing him as well as a possible money trail.

She didn't have money for an attorney. Hell, she didn't have money to spare for the cabs she'd taken that day. Worse, she couldn't cancel her late-night shopping order because it would look like she was trying to cover her tracks. Definitely didn't have the money for that.

Maybe she could get a second job. But as what? And when would she take classes?

What she wouldn't give to walk away from it all. Nothing was keeping her there.

Well, school. And Gretchen.

Okay, school was a joke. Why had she majored in European History? What could she possibly do with that degree once she graduated? At least Gretchen was pre-law. Once she was licensed to practice, she probably wouldn't have the time for Rina. She'd be incredibly busy, and then they'd run in different circles.

No. Rina's family was gone. She'd soon lose her best friend. She had no future. Nothing keeping her there.

Well, nothing but a possible conviction in her future.

What she needed was a miracle.

What she needed was Damien.

Gretchen nudged her. "Well?"

With her thoughts careening through her head, she'd missed what her friend had asked her. "Well, what?"

"Were you even listening to me? Of course you weren't. You had that same look you get when one of the customers gets too grabby. Like you go to your special happy place in your mind to block it all out."

Special happy place? If only. "I was just thinking about what the detective said."

"That's what I've been talking about!"

Rina sighed. "I'm going home. I need a nap before work."

"All right." Gretchen glared at her, but at least she stopped yammering. "I'm just going to run into the drug store and buy—"

A lift of one eyebrow was all Rina needed to silence her.

"I forgot. Geez. My nerves are shot. I picked the worst possible day to quit smoking."

"You're right. You should have quit years ago. In fact, you never should have started."

After a thick silence, Gretchen rooted in her purse and pulled out a stick of gum. "This isn't going to cut it. Maybe I'll go buy a patch or nicotine gum or something."

"Save your money. We can't afford to squander any extra coin right now."

Her friend started walking away without even saying goodbye. She chomped on her gum and muttered something Rina couldn't quite hear. Probably for the best. It was bound to be something nasty about her, anyway.

Rina crossed the street and hurried home. When she saw the broken glass in her bedroom, she sighed and walked back out to the living room. Snuggling under a blanket on her sofa, she drifted into an exhausted, albeit restless, sleep.

❖

Rina's nap somehow made her even more tired. Her time would have been better spent repairing her window and getting ready for work. Instead, she tossed and turned, woke up late, then had to rush to get ready. She got to Bar Belles twenty minutes late, and they were already slammed.

"Where the hell were you?" Gretchen asked when their paths crossed by the bar. She hadn't even gone one day without smoking and was already uber-irritable.

"I slept in. Sorry. Why are there so many people here tonight?"

"Larry decided to run a pizza-and-pilsner special. Surprised you didn't see the sign in the window."

"I came in the back. And since when did Larry run sales on anything?"

Gretchen hefted her tray and turned toward the crowd. "Since he doesn't like the new brand of beer he ordered and the freezer is too full to store much more food. He's been talking to the distributor about a new brand of egg roll."

When Gretchen walked away from the bar, at least three of the patrons grabbed her ass. Rina sighed. It was going to be a long and miserable night. She grabbed her own tray and started to take and distribute orders among the customers.

About two hours into her shift, her back ached and her toes felt like they might break off. Just half an hour until her break. Assuming Larry let her take it then. The crowd hadn't thinned at all, and it looked like it wasn't going to.

Rina swiped sweat off her brow with the back of her hand and made her way into the throng to take another round of orders. She had a table in the back corner, furthest from the stage, which was usually her favorite zone. Most of the troublemakers sat as close to the dancers as possible, where most of the shy and timid men sat in the shadows in the back. She plastered another fake smile on her face and sauntered up to the customer tucked into the darkness.

The smile faded from Rina's face when she saw who sat at the table, sneering at her.

Dylan Ramer. And a few of his friends.

"You shouldn't be here." Her voice had a tremor she hoped he couldn't hear over the music.

"Free country." He leered at her, his gaze traveling down her body and back, lingering on her breasts.

She swallowed and crossed her arms. "We're not supposed to have any contact with each other. The police—"

"The police don't believe a word you said. Even if they did, they wouldn't do anything about it. I'm connected in this town. You... aren't." Ramer trailed his fingers over her hip, and she shifted away from him. He grabbed her wrist, yanked her down to his eye-level, then twisted her arm until she had no choice but to sit on his lap. He gyrated in his seat and tugged her back against his chest. His rancid breath blew wisps of her hair as he whispered in her ear. "Aw, don't be that way, babe. I think I know a way we can settle this out of court."

He held her captive, her body pressed against his. She felt his interest grow between them, and a chill ran down her spine. The room spun, her stomach churned. Frantic, she scanned the room for help. The customers all had their backs toward her, their gazes directed at the dancers. Tiny stood by the stage, and his staff lingered near the private rooms and main entrance. No one could see her in the dark corner.

No one would hear her scream over the beat of the bass.

"You and me," Ramer said, "we're going to get up and make our way to one of the private rooms."

She shook her head, unable to speak as tears rolled down her cheeks.

"Oh, yes. We're going right now. You're going to strip for me, then I'm going to fuck you senseless." He grasped her chin then jerked her head toward him. "After I'm satisfied, you're gonna do my friends."

She couldn't make out their features in the darkness and

didn't think she'd want to. Better not to react. Better not to know.

Maybe better to pass out and hope someone noticed before he got his way. She willed herself to check out, to slip into unconsciousness, but oblivion didn't come.

"Make it good, and I'll let you live. Hell, I'll even tell the cops it was all a misunderstanding." He reached around her, squeezed her breast until she whimpered from the pain. "Leave me or my boys unsatisfied, and we'll make sure you pay, good and slow. We'll get you one way or another, might as well come willingly. I know you don't want to die. And I don't think you want to rot in prison for the next twenty years. A sweet piece of ass like you?" He slid his hand down between her legs then pushed up, grinding his palm against her. "You wouldn't last a night before you became someone's girlfriend. What do you think is worse? One night with us or twenty years with... well, who knows?"

She struggled to get away, but his grip was too tight. He stood, hauling her to her feet in front of him, then started dragging her toward the private rooms. His guys flanked him, blocking her view of Tiny or any of the house security. Her breath came in shallow gasps, her vision darkened.

He'd have to force himself on her because she wouldn't go to him willingly. In a minute, she might not even be conscious.

A looming shadow darkened the entry to the private rooms. She blinked, tried to clear her vision. Tiny?

"Release her."

That deep baritone, that massive size.

She looked up and squinted at her savior.

Damien.

Five

Rage roiled through Damien at the site of his precious Rina in the clutches of that swine. If the bastard didn't unhand her—immediately—Damien would rip the guy's arms off at the shoulder then club him to death with his severed limbs.

"Well, look who it is. Not so tough now that I have backup, are you?"

"Who is this asshole, Ramer?" One of the lackeys stepped forward, eying Damien head-to-toe and back.

"The fool I was telling you about. From last night." Ramer released his grip on Rina, and she weaved on her feet.

Damien grabbed her before she hit the floor. "Are you okay?" He only tore his gaze from Ramer and his thugs for a moment, and then only to look her over when she didn't answer. Satisfied she was physically unscathed, he shoved her behind him.

Ramer's goons closed ranks while he fished in his pocket for his phone. After placing a call, he held it inches from Damien's face and sneered. "I'll get back to her later. This is an opportunity I can't pass up. Cops want to talk to you."

"Problem here?"

Damien glanced to his side. Tiny and three other bouncers stood there, fists clenched at their sides.

"Nothing I can't handle," Damien said.

"Just because you can doesn't mean you have to."

Even in the dim lighting, Damien could see the color had drained from Ramer's face. He disconnected the call while it was still ringing, shoved his phone back into his pocket, then nodded to his friends. They gave the bouncers a wide berth as they slithered around them, headed to the door.

Once he'd passed Damien, Ramer turned around, looked at him, then Rina, then back. "Don't think this is over. These guys won't always have your back."

"I didn't need them last night. Won't need them next time, either."

Ramer bumped into a chair, then he turned and hurried after his friends.

"That's a hell of a thank you," Tiny said.

"I told you I didn't need your help." Damien bristled. Like he couldn't protect Rina on his own.

"And like I said, just because you can do something doesn't mean you have to do it alone."

Rina placed her hand on Tiny's arm, looked at him and the rest of the bouncers. "Well, I appreciate you coming to my rescue. Thank you."

The other guys nodded and dispersed. Tiny stayed. "You okay?"

She nodded. "I'm fine."

He met Damien's gaze, but he still spoke to her. "I'm here for you. Anything you need. Anything at all."

"It's okay, Tiny. You can go. Tell Larry I'm taking my break."

He still stared at Damien. "I'll go with you."

"No. Go back to work. I'm fine."

Tiny looked at her. "I'm going to call the cops, file a report."

"No, you're not. They won't care. Ramer's gone. He left no evidence. There's no point."

"The cameras may have picked up... something."

Damien knew Tiny didn't want to give voice to anything that had happened. Didn't blame him. He couldn't even think about it without the fury consuming him.

"Tiny. Let it go. It's too dark back in this corner for our cameras. It's over. I'm okay."

His jaw ticked, then his expression softened. "Where are you taking your break?"

"Go back to the stage, Tiny."

Tiny patted her shoulder, shot one last glare at Damien, then turned away.

Damn it, but he was a good guy. Good to Rina. A man of worth. Damien closed his eyes, took a deep breath. "Hey," he called after him. "Tiny."

Tiny turned, glared, but didn't speak.

"Thank you."

The bouncer's expression softened. He nodded and waved before making his way through the crowd.

Damien turned his attention back to Rina. She was steady on her feet but didn't look well.

"I need some fresh air," she said. "Care to join me?"

She couldn't stop him with a vat of burning pitch. He followed her around the tables and out the front door.

He watched her pace in tiny circles under the harsh glow of the streetlight. A ponytail held her hair back, but a few tendrils had come loose. The soft curls framed her face, adding a softness to her already exquisite features.

When she stopped pacing and faced him, he didn't expect the hardened expression. She stood, hands on hips, foot tapping a rapid beat, and looked up to meet his gaze.

"I suppose I should thank you for stepping in, but I'm so angry with you right now, I—"

"What? You're angry with me? What did I do?"

"What did you do? You're joking, right?" Her voice grew shrill, and she stomped her foot. "This is all your fault!" She shoved him.

Surprised and unprepared, he stumbled back a step. Forget a woman scorned. Apparently a woman angry over... Well, he didn't know what prompted the anger. But he knew the reference to the fury of hell and understood the adage.

Not having the first clue what to say, he said nothing. Just waited for her to continue.

An unladylike growl escaped her lips, and she whirled away from him. Looking up, she took a deep breath then let it out slowly. When she turned, she'd calmed, and she addressed him with quiet deliberation. "Damien, you owe me an explanation. And you aren't going to disappear this time. Not until you've answered all my questions."

Talk about a change in tactics. He'd braced for another attack, and instead got a calm, chilly discussion. One he hadn't expected and didn't want.

"I don't know what you want from me." That was true enough.

"I want to know where you came from last night. And tonight. What do you have to do with all of this?"

"I have nothing to do with any of this. I just wanted to help."

"The police are looking for you. They think Gretchen and I concocted this whole story."

He shook his head. "I don't understand. Why would they think that?"

"Because that's what Ramer told them. He said we stole money from him. That when he resisted, we used you to rough him up to get what we wanted. They're going through our finances, asking us questions. I looked guilty because I couldn't direct them to you!"

"Just tell them the truth."

"Don't you think I tried that? They still want to speak with you."

"Do you want me to leave town?"

"Are you insane?" Her voice grew shrill again.

Maybe he was crazy, because he hadn't any idea what to say to her, what to do for her. "How can I help?"

"How can you—? I just told you. Talk to the police!"

That was the last thing he wanted to do. He would defend her to his dying breath, whatever that meant for a creature like him. But the authorities? What would he say to them? What would they want from him? He stood there, blinking, uncertain of what to do next.

Rina took another deep breath, then she placed her hand on his arm. "Damien, I need your help. You might be the only hope I have of clearing my name."

He shook his head. "I don't want to speak to the police. Maybe I could just take you away from all this." How? Fly her somewhere on his ridged back? What the hell was he thinking?

"I can't leave." A strange look he couldn't identify crossed her face. "Not now. I'd look guilty. I have to prove what Ramer did to me. If you'd just talk to the—Why are you shaking your head?" Her eyes widened, and she dropped her voice to a whisper. "Are you wanted by the police?"

He saw the fear in her eyes, and he wanted to reassure her. He'd never been a dishonest man. But how to prove it to her? Talking to the police was out of the question. He didn't even have an identity. What would he say to them? That he was a gargoyle who spent his days on Nathaniel Burton Mansion, and at night, after he came to life, his battle instincts kicked in, which was how he'd been in a position to save her? They'd lock him up.

Wonder what they'd think if he was in a cell and turned into stone.

"Damien, please?" She stepped away but still met his gaze. "I have to tell them something. Why you were there. Where you live. Where you work. What you do." She took a deep breath. "I don't even know your last name."

If he didn't worry about the ramifications, he'd sprout his wings and fly away. What had Anael been thinking? Damien didn't see how he could ever make this work. It was too complicated. He couldn't even give her the simplest of answers.

Flop sweat took him by surprise, and he struggled for a response. Any response.

"Well, I'll be. Damien? Is that you?"

Damien turned to see who was speaking. It was all he could do to keep quiet when Anael stepped into the glow of the streetlight—wearing black jeans and a cable knit sweater the same green color as his usual tunic. He wasn't glowing like Damien had often seen him, but his appearance was so strange, he drew more attention than if his body lit up like the light bulb above them. He seemed far too handsome to be human, and Damien worried Rina would be suspicious.

Or enamored.

"Damien Stone," Anael said. "It is you. How've you been? It's been ages. What? Three, no four years, I think."

He stuck out his hand, and Damien took it. The angel shook it with more force than necessary, and he had to flex his fingers when Anael let go.

"But where are my manners?" Anael turned to Rina and extended his hand. "Al DeAngelo."

Rina looked as confused and surprised as Damien felt, but she also shook Anael's hand in greeting. "Katarina Whitman."

"Katarina. A pleasure."

"So, tell me, Al." She shot Damien a saccharine grin before

turning her attention to Anael. "How do you two know each other?"

"Oh, we met ages ago in France. Our boy here was fighting a losing battle. Didn't look like he was going to get out of there in one piece, so I stepped in and offered him an alternative."

Damien glared at him. Didn't matter that he offered no specifics. He spoke the truth. Or a version of it. A truth Damien obviously couldn't share.

"Business can be like war." Anael looked pointedly at Damien. "Glad to have run into you now, though. I lost your number a while back. It's good to see you again."

Damien continued to scowl at the angel, who took no notice. Instead, he turned his attention to Rina and offered her a dazzling smile.

"What kind of business are you in, Al?" she asked.

"Oh, I dabble in many things. But enough about me. Tell me about the beautiful Katarina."

She blushed. "My friends call me Rina."

"Well, Rina, I hope to be included in that group."

"Of course."

He linked her arm through his and began a slow stroll away from Damien. "Perhaps you'll let me take you both out for a drink. I'd love to catch up with Damien. And get to know you better. Rina."

Her name flowed off his lips like honey in tea, thick and warm and sweet. Damien hated it.

She looked at her watch. "I'd really love to, but I have to get back to work. Rain check?"

"Just name the time and place."

After she shook his hand again, she turned to Damien. "Will you be here at closing?"

"I don't know what more you want to discuss."

"If nothing else, I'd like to know Tiny has backup if Ramer comes back."

Somethings about women didn't change through the centuries. They still knew how to manipulate men.

He sighed. "I'll be around."

"Don't disappoint me." She walked inside.

⚜

When the door closed Rina inside Bar Belles, Damien rounded on Anael. "What's the matter with you?"

"You looked like you needed some help."

"Help, sure. My whole life's history blurted out on a street corner? Not so much."

"I didn't tell her any specifics. You couldn't even give her your name."

"That's because people don't go by their places of birth any longer."

"Which is why I gave you a fill-in."

"Stone? How original. *Al.*"

Anael shrugged. "If the horns and wings fit."

Damien glared at him.

"I'm not supposed to interfere, but—"

"That didn't stop you earlier."

"I'll pretend you didn't just interrupt me. Unless, of course, you don't want this?" He reached into his pocket, pulled out a wallet, then waved it at Damien.

"What am I going to do with that?"

"Most people need money to travel, buy dinner, whatever. You'll certainly need ID when you talk to the police. You should have conjured them when you transformed, but I supposed you didn't think about that."

"Money? ID?"

"Identification. Like I said, I shouldn't interfere, but this stuff is a necessity these days. When you transform for now on, think this into reality with you like you do your clothes." Anael tossed him the wallet.

Damien snatched the leather folio from the air. He had wondered about the clothes. That was one mystery solved. Appearently he *conjured* them. Whatever the hell that meant. He looked at the angel. "And this is you not interfering?"

"If you'd conjured it yourself, I wouldn't have had to. Besides, I'm really more bending the rules than breaking them."

Damien looked through the contents of the wallet. Thousands of dollars plus an ID with the name "Damien Stone" and the address of the mansion on it. "And what happens when someone knocks at the door of the manse? The ruse will be blown."

"Shouldn't be an issue. I've dealt with that, too."

"How? Did you transform someone to look like me? Alter people's memories?"

"Hardly anything so difficult. I've made it appear that no one is home. The mansion will remain dark and locked to anyone outside it. And to anyone inside, no doorbell, knock, or shout will be heard."

"Well, Al, you've thought of everything."

"I try to be thorough."

"You missed one detail, though. I have no story to give Rina. Or the police."

He didn't wait for a reply. There was nothing Anael could say to make things better, anyway. Despite knowing the angel could catch him if he wanted to, Damien transformed into the grotesque monster he felt like and flew away.

Damien soared over Pittsburgh, watching the traffic back up at the tunnels and Station Square bustle with activity. He took a dip in the Monongahela and smiled at the giant catfish waiting underwater for a surprise snack. So many people thought there were monsters down there. But they were just giant fish.

The real monster flew above them every nightfall, but no one even suspected.

How could he possibly move on with Rina when he didn't fit in with her world?

He'd just have to figure out a way to keep her safe without actually being in her life.

And if that meant losing even the pitiful life he led, so be it. She deserved better than Damien Stone—statue by day, creature by night.

No, his world might be boring and predictable, but it didn't result in anyone getting harmed. And he'd be damned —he'd literally be damned and didn't care—if he couldn't protect Katarina Whitman.

He flew around until he dried off, then he headed to Bar Belles. A promise was a promise. He'd given his word. Ramer could reappear, and he needed to be sure she was safe.

Damien watched the building for several hours until someone turned off the garish fluorescent name sign, flipped the placard on the door to CLOSED, and turned off the interior lights. Rina would be outside soon. He flew to the back alley. The shadows provided him with cover while he began the painful process of changing into a human.

Transformation complete, he stretched to get the kinks out of his joints, checked his pocket for the wallet and money Anael had provided, then watched the door.

While he waited, he could plan his speech to Rina.

But try as he might, he couldn't find the words.

Damien found her more beautiful every time he saw her. She'd let her hair down, letting it cascade over her shoulders in a riot of blonde curls, and she'd reapplied her makeup. No one would ever know she worked a difficult job into the wee hours of the night. She looked fresh and vibrant.

He wanted nothing more than to pull her into his arms, fly her over the city, then kiss her all night long.

Instead, he steeled his resolve. His past was too complicated. His future uncertain. He had nothing to offer her. Best to just talk to the police, convince them of her innocence, then say goodbye.

There had to be better words for that. Something eloquent and convincing. Something she could neither argue nor overrule.

But nothing came to him.

She waved goodbye to Tiny and Gretchen, neither of whom looked too happy that she approached him rather than going with them. He waved a half-hearted greeting, and Gretchen waved back. Tiny merely nodded, then they walked away, presumably toward a vehicle or bus stop. Rina hurried toward him with a smile on her face. "I didn't think you'd show."

"I'm offended. I always keep my word. Why would you think otherwise?"

"Well, I don't have a good track record with men. With anyone, really. And you seemed so evasive earlier."

"Yes, well..." Come on, words. Something, anything, to get her to back off. But nothing came to him.

"Look, Damien, I think maybe we just need to get something out of the way, then we can move on to other things."

"What?" Her beauty blinded him. He couldn't think straight, couldn't find the words or the willpower to walk away.

She stepped closer to him.

What was she doing? What did she want? What did they need to get out of the way? Details of his name? His occupation?

His thoughts reeled with panic, confusion, worst-case scenarios.

She stood toe-to-toe with him, gazed up into his eyes. He

saw the light dusting of freckles across her nose and cheek-bones, heard her sharp intake of breath.

Was she as nervous as he? Why?

Then she kissed him.

And he couldn't think at all.

Six

That first instant when her lips met his, she panicked.
His unyielding mouth, his stiff body, his lack of
response... it all made her think she'd made a huge
mistake.

That moment lasted a lifetime. And only a fraction of a
second.

Before shame made her pull away, he wrapped his arms
around her and pulled her tight to him. She felt every hard
plane of his chiseled body, every exhale of his warm breath,
every desire he held in check. He trembled with restraint.

And she reveled in it.

Despite his hard visage, his lips were soft, his embrace
gentle. When he deepened the kiss, his tongue first teasing her
mouth open then exploring hers with lingering leisure, she
nearly melted.

Seriously, if he hadn't been holding her, she'd be a puddle
on the ground.

He swept her along in a maelstrom of passion and
emotions, and she was helpless to do anything other than ride
the wave. When he nipped her lip, she yipped and broke the

kiss, stumbling back. Her eyelids fluttered open, and she had to blink a few times to clear her vision.

She swore she saw...

No. That was ridiculous. Humans didn't have wings. She shook her head, buried the thought.

When Damien reached for her, she cringed, and he dropped his hand.

"I'm sorry," he said. "I got carried away."

"There's no reason to be sorry. I started the kiss. If anything, I owe you an apology."

He scoffed. "Believe me. It wasn't a hardship."

Rina didn't know what to make of that, so she didn't reply. Instead, she rubbed her lip, remembering the sensation of his teeth nibbling on the tender tissue.

She'd never felt anything so erotic in her life.

"Did I hurt you?" His voice was low, soft. His eyes dark, like storm clouds or shadows.

"What? No, why?"

He touched his own lip. She realized what he must be thinking and lowered her hand to her side. "Definitely not hurt. Just... just remembering. Fondly." Despite feeling her cheeks flush, she smiled at him and held his gaze. Her smile only faltered a moment when she remembered the image of wings.

"Are you sure?" His gaze roamed over her, and he seemed to probe deep into her soul.

Not wanting to give any more ground, she turned her head and looked up and down the street. "Well." Her voice cracked and she cleared her throat and began again. "Now that we got that out of the way, let's get down to business."

"Business?"

"Yes. I told you. I need you to talk to the police. Do you think maybe tomorrow morning you could—"

"No."

His voice was so sharp, his tone so matter-of-fact, she recoiled from him.

"I'm sorry. I'm unavailable most mornings. If you want me to talk to someone, perhaps we can do it now?"

"Now? It's almost three in the morning."

"Given the hours you work, I would think you could understand when a person is only available during certain times of the day."

"And what is it exactly that you do?"

He hesitated a moment, and Rina wondered again what he did. Was it illegal? Was it something that embarrassed him? Something he was contractually obligated to keep secret?

"I'm in security. My obligations during the day are, well, let's say they're set in stone. I can't get away. For any reason. If you want me to speak with the police, it will have to be in the evening."

"Okay. Well, I still think it's rather late to call the detective. I'm sure he's not even on duty now. How about early tomorrow evening?"

"That will be fine. Now, as Tiny is long gone and Ramer could be anywhere, would you permit me to see you home?"

They weren't done making plans for Damien to meet Detective Urbani, but the mere mention of Ramer took her thoughts in another direction. He could be out there. Anywhere. And Tiny and the rest of the bouncers were already gone. Despite knowing next to nothing about Damien, she felt safe with him, and she'd welcome his protection.

And his company.

She linked her arm through his and began walking toward her apartment. Whether she'd ask him in or not remained to be seen. She'd surely sleep better—or at all—knowing he was there to keep her safe. On the other hand, she'd never been dependent on a man before. Besides, Damien didn't guarantee she'd sleep. She could think of plenty of things that would keep her up. All. Night. Long.

Rina didn't know what to do. But she knew which way she was leaning.

⁘

"This is me," Rina said.

They'd made light and easy conversation during the walk home, and she couldn't believe they'd already traveled the few miles to her apartment. She hadn't even gotten around to asking for his number to schedule the meeting with the detective.

Hadn't decided if she wanted to ask him up, either.

"Right here?" Damien gestured toward the building they were standing in front of.

Rina shook her head and nodded at the building across the street. She looked up at the plastic covering her broken window. "No, here. The unit with the broken window."

He frowned. "How long has that been broken? You should call the building manager."

She didn't want to tell him that she'd broken it, so she'd have to repair it. It would cost enough on her own. No point in paying the up-charge for labor and materials the realty management company would undoubtedly charge.

Instead of answering him, she studied the window. One corner of the plastic film flapped in the breeze. She could barely tell in the shadow of the fire escape, but if she squinted, she could make it out. The corner had come loose. First thing in the morning, she definitely needed to deal with the repair.

He released her arm, faced her, then looked down into her eyes. "I'm glad the walk was uneventful. Perhaps Ramer is all talk, and now he'll leave you alone."

"Wouldn't that be nice?" His gaze was hypnotic, but she needed to think clearly so she looked away. Again she glanced up at her apartment and cursed herself for forgetting to leave a light on. The last thing she wanted was to walk into her home while it was dark. While her window wasn't repaired. While her home wasn't secure and her life was still in danger.

She wanted Damien to walk her up. Wanted to ask him in. To feel safe in her own apartment and sleep without worry.

And she wanted the opportunity to avoid sleep for a much more exhilarating reason than fear.

Just as she was about to extend an invitation, Damien spoke.

"Well, it's pretty late. I'll wait until you get inside. Just turn on your light so I know you're safe."

She sighed. Missed that opportunity. And didn't have the nerve to circle back around to it.

"You might want to think about leaving a light on."

Beat him to that thought.

His stare bore into her, and he hesitated a moment.

Was he going to kiss her again? She leaned a little toward him. How she wanted another kiss, after which would be the perfect opportunity to ask him up.

Instead, though, he backed away and put his hands in his pockets. "Hurry, now. You need your rest."

Was that a compliment or an insult? Unsure, she didn't answer him. She just half-heartedly waved goodbye and jogged across the street.

She was halfway up to her apartment when she realized she hadn't obtained his phone number. Nor had they settled on a time for the meeting. Maybe she should go back down.

But she was tired, and it was late. She'd just call down to him from the window once she got inside.

Maybe she could ask him up then. To talk about the arrangements for the following evening, of course. Clever. Good plan. A smile crept across her face.

Yeah. No one would notice her yelling down five stories to

invite a hunk of a man up to her apartment. She shook her head at her stupidity.

Then Rina decided she didn't care. There weren't many people out at that time of night. She didn't know the ones who were and didn't care if they judged her. Besides, she didn't want to be alone.

When she got to her apartment, she unlocked the door then slipped inside. She didn't want him to leave before she got to the window to call down to him, so she left off her light. Navigating the room in the dark was easy. She didn't have much furniture, and everything had been in the same spots for years. Just before she reached the window, she was grabbed from behind.

The hand on her face muffled her scream, and the other hand dug into her soft flesh. She struggled against the unseen attacker. Hot breath wafted past her ear, and she recognized the putrid smell.

Dylan Ramer had her in his filthy clutches. He had her, and she was alone and defenseless.

That thought raced through her mind as fear fired through every fiber of her being. She bit at his hand.

He released her mouth and wrapped his arm tightly around her, squeezing her ribs in a painful, crushing grasp.

Her shriek echoed through the apartment when he tackled her.

⁜

Rina fought against her panic, fought against the grip Ramer had on her, but she was losing both battles. She screamed again, softer than the first time, and he backhanded her. Tears streamed down her cheeks.

He pinned her to the floor and laughed. "Not so brave without your goons backing you up, huh? I'm going to enjoy this. I'm going to make you pray for death, but I'm not going to grant your wish. I'm going to let you live with the constant reminder of who had the last laugh. I'll just make sure you can't talk about it afterward."

She gasped for breath. "You'll never get away with it. You're just giving me ammunition for my case against you."

He laughed again. "I have an alibi. I'm across town, playing poker with my buddies. At least five people can vouch for me. Which makes you a liar and makes me untouch—" His hold slackened, and he looked behind him, tilting his head like he listened for something.

Her heart had been pounding too hard to hear anything other than his psychotic rants. Dare she hope he'd get up to check things? Maybe run away? Or release his hold a little more so she could escape?

Before she could grasp at any unrealistic hope, he clamped his fingers tight around her wrists again. "Now—"

Then he sailed across the room. Rina heard a thud and a snap before Ramer howled in pain. Noise of a scuffle ensued. The crack of punches landed, the thud of impacts on the walls and floor, the shattering of pottery, the panting of exertion, the grunting of pain... all the sounds held her in paralyzed shock. When something whizzed past her head, she snapped out of her stupor and scuttled on her hands and knees toward a table to turn on a lamp. Shards of something broken sliced her palms and knees, but she pressed on, only to find the lamp wasn't there.

Of course. The shards were pottery fragments from the base of the lamp. And probably the light bulb.

She pushed to her feet and hurried toward the kitchen, thinking even light from the adjoining room would help. If she could just avoid the flailing arms and legs from the battle in the middle of her apartment. Or anything else they threw at each other.

By the time she got to her kitchen and flipped the switch, the racket had subsided. When the pale light illuminated her living room, all she saw was Damien, standing amid the wreckage of her apartment, blood dripping down the side of his face. Her apartment door stood ajar.

"Are you okay?" He eyed her carefully, assessing her with concern even though his tone was brusque.

"I'm fine. I'm fine." Was she repeating it for his benefit or hers?

"You aren't fine. You're bleeding."

She looked down. Blood dripped from her palms to the floor, from her knees down her legs. "Just scratches. I'm okay."

"You sure?"

She nodded.

"Then I'm going after him. Call the police." He headed toward the door.

"Damien, wait. You're bleeding, too. Worse than me."

He touched his face and looked at the blood on his hands. His brow furrowed, and he squinted at his fingers.

"Damien? Do you need to sit? Does blood make you squeamish?" God, don't let him collapse. She'd never be able to catch him.

"Does blood—?" He snorted. "No. I just didn't realize I was cut. Now, I have to go. He's getting away." Again, he started to leave.

"Damien, please. Don't leave me."

He glanced at the door then turned back toward her.

"He's gone by now. Just sit. Stay with me."

This time he looked at her first, then the door.

"Maybe these are worse than I thought." She looked at her hands.

He rushed to her side, helped her through the rubble to her dinette set. As soon as he righted a chair, he gently guided her onto it. "Let me see."

When he bent his head over her hands to study them, she smiled. Her wounds weren't too bad, but she'd used the injuries to get him to stay. Which he did, proving he cared.

"Rina, do you have a first aid kit?"

"The bathroom. I'll get it." She started to rise, but he held her down.

"No. I'll go." Damien rose, wiped his face with the bottom of his shirt.

Despite all the drama of the evening, she couldn't help but admire his chiseled abs when she glimpsed them.

"You better call the police," he said.

"What's the point? They don't believe me. They won't believe me. Ramer said his friends are going to give him an alibi."

"There needs to be a record of this attack. It will add to your case."

"Or it will make me look like even more of a liar."

He crossed his arms over his massive chest. "Are you going to call, or am I?"

Rina sighed, recognizing the stubborn male demeanor for what it was—impossible to counter. She grabbed her phone while he went into her bathroom.

She dialed 911. After a brief explanation and several assurances that she was in no immediate danger, she ended the call. By then, Damien was back with the first aid kit.

He knelt in front of her then took her hand.

And took her breath away.

There was something so intimate about a man kneeling at a woman's feet. Damien at her feet? Almost carnal.

After he stared into her eyes for what felt like eternity, he lowered his head and studied her palm. Then he got to work. He sterilized tweezers with alcohol and proceeded to extract every sliver in her right hand, then her left. When he finished that, he wiped both palms with another wipe, put a non-stick bandage on each one, then wrapped them both in gauze.

His efforts couldn't have been more intimate. Or so she thought before he pressed his lips to each palm. She had to blink back tears. No one had ever been so gentle with her. So kind. So tender.

"Now your knees." His voice—deep, husky—barely registered.

Rina snapped out of the luxurious fog she'd been steeped in. A glance down at her knees caused her to realize she'd have to slip out of her stockings for him to help her. How was she going to deal with that? Maybe she'd just rip through the runs already in the thin hose. That would expose her flesh without her stripping in front of him. Or she could slip into her bedroom and change into shorts. Had she even shaved her legs that morning? Maybe it would be best to handle the first aid herself.

He made the decision for her.

First he slipped off one of her shoes. He ran his thumb across the arch, sending tingles shooting up her leg and into her core. She tipped her head back and closed her eyes, just simmering in the sensation of his hands on her body. Then he removed her other shoe, again massaging the sole of her foot. Her body began a slow burn, and she lifted her head to meet his gaze.

He stared into her eyes, into her soul. She was fully clothed, minus her shoes, but she felt stripped bare.

And loved it.

Damien slid his palms up her leg, under her skirt. His gaze never left hers, and for that she was grateful, because her breasts heaved with her breathlessness, and certainly her face had flushed.

There was something so sensual about his rough fingers skimming her soft skin, lowering the silky hose down her leg. When he pulled the garment over her knee, where the blood had seeped into the stockings and matted the material to her wounds, she barely felt the tug of separation.

All she felt was heat. Everywhere.

He finished removing the stocking, then took the same exquisite time removing the second.

Her skirt had ridden up, and his hands caressed her bare thighs. It would take so little for him to slide his hands just a little further. Just a little higher.

Before her fantasies ran away from her, he started plucking glass out of her knees. The sting barely registered but was enough to bring her back to reality.

Bending over her, he worked diligently until every shard was removed, then he cleaned and bandaged her wounds.

Rina was all too aware of where his head was, where his hands were, how a shift of her hips and a small spread of her legs would be an easy invitation.

She bit her lip. Did she dare?

Before she made up her mind, he stood and put the kit back together. "I better put this away." His voice cracked. He grabbed the kit then hurried off to the bathroom.

Could it be? Was he as nervous as she was? As turned on?

He was gone for a while, much longer than it would have taken to replace the kit under the sink. Maybe he *was* as affected as she had been. Maybe he needed a moment to compose himself, too. A small smile crossed her lips as she considered the impact she had on him. She'd never felt so powerful, so desirable. So sexy.

When he came back out, he'd cleaned the blood off his face, and a sheen of ointment glistened over his wound.

Her ego deflated, her smile fled.

He wasn't affected by her body. He was tending to his.

She rose and turned away from him before he saw her mortification. "I guess I can clean up while we wait." She headed for the kitchen, but he grabbed her arm and spun her to face him. Before she could argue, he embraced her. She felt his arms tremble, heard him draw a ragged breath.

She sunk into him, glad he was there, thrilled he cared,

relieved to finally be able to relax. He was with her, holding her. Ramer was gone. Damien had saved her.

At the moment, nothing else mattered.

Was it seconds? Minutes? Hours? She didn't know. Honestly, she could have stayed in his embrace forever. But he backed away, and she felt cold without his arms around her.

Not knowing what to say, what to do, she turned again to the kitchen. "I can probably have most of this mess swept up before the police get here."

Again, he grabbed her arm. "That's evidence. Leave it alone."

She bit her lip, stood and looked around the room, uncertain what to do.

He pulled her closer, guided them to the sofa, then tugged her down to join him.

"They'll be here soon. We'll get this all taken care of."

Nothing would feel better than to sink back into his embrace, but the buzzer rang, signaling a visitor downstairs. Probably the police. Finally.

And wasn't she more than a little glad Damien had stopped things before they started?

She rose and crossed the room to the intercom. "Hello?"

"Detective Urbani."

Detective Urbani? What was he doing there? She expected uniformed officers, not him. She bit her lip, afraid to ponder the implications of his arrival.

He rang again.

Rina spoke into the unit on the wall. "Come on up." Then she used the remote unlock feature to buzz him in.

After opening the door a crack, she turned to Damien. "I guess we don't have to schedule an appointment with the detective tomorrow. Looks like he's here."

Seven

~

Damien studied the detective. The guy looked polished. Suit and vest, no tie. Shined shoes, groomed hair. For someone who supposedly worked the day shift—and for the late hour of the night—he was way too put together. Under different circumstances, that would be commendable. Damien always appreciated a strong work ethic and the ability to perform at a moment's notice.

But not when it was used against him and so much was at stake.

Rina's freedom and his life were on the line. If Urbani did his job, then they wouldn't have a problem. But if he was all surface and no substance—worse still, if he was bought off—Damien would have to get Rina to safety, far from this town and Ramer's ever-present threats. Somewhere far away.

He didn't have the time or means to travel traditionally. He'd have to take her at night, in his *other* form.

Which would reveal him for the monster he was. And what was the likelihood she'd prefer a literal beast over a figurative one?

"Have a seat, Detective." Rina gestured to her sofa.

"Think I'll have a look around first. If you don't mind."

"Not at all." She shrugged at Damien behind the detective's back.

Damien followed Urbani around the small apartment, trying to assess the man's competence. He had to admit, the guy was thorough. Officers photographed what the detective pointed out, bagged and tagged what he told them to. He didn't seem to miss a thing.

Which meant his interview skills would likely be just as thorough. Was that good or bad?

Urbani turned around and narrowly avoided bumping into Damien. "Got something you want to add?"

Damien crossed his arms. "Not especially."

The detective gestured to the living room. "Too bad. We need your statement. Take a seat."

Rina wrung her bandaged hands and paced in small circles. Then she looked at the detective, who sat in the lone chair in the room. "Can I get you a drink? Water? Coffee? Are you hungry?"

Urbani raised an eyebrow and smirked. Damien understood that. He also thought maybe the stress had gotten to her. It wasn't a tea party, for Pete's sake.

"No, thank you."

"Well, I'd like one." She retreated to the kitchen and returned with a bottle of wine and three glasses. "Help yourself, if you're so inclined." Then she poured herself a full glass and downed half of it in two gulps.

The detective's eyes widened, but he didn't comment. "Shall we start?"

She shrugged and sat beside Damien. He wanted to take her hand but thought better of it. Who knew how that small gesture might be interpreted.

"So, Miss Whitman. Why don't you tell me what happened here tonight?"

Rina took a deep breath then launched into her story. Damien knew all those details already. When she entered her building, he flew to the rooftop across the street from her. He expected her to turn on the light, but instead he heard her scream. It only took a second for him to fly across the street and let himself in her plastic-covered window. Probably how that bastard got in, too. The fire escape landing was right under that window. Wouldn't have taken much for Ramer to get up there. Damn it, why didn't he walk her up, see her to her apartment safely? But he was afraid of what she would think of him if he'd be so forward to ask. Worse if he'd insisted. There was the matter of her virtue. Not that it seemed to be as important in this century as it had been in his.

Given he'd taken advantage of her injuries just to put his hands on her, he had to wonder what kind of hero he really was. Not much of one, apparently.

He tuned back in to the interview. Turned his thoughts back to Ramer and the danger he posed.

Rina hesitated only briefly when asked if she knew who attacked her. Damien knew she was worried about Ramer's claim of an alibi and the detective believing her. But he was proud of her courage. She told the truth.

Urbani took several notes, then turned to Damien. "And you swooped in and saved her?"

If only he knew how accurate that statement was. "I did."

"And you are?"

"Damien Stone."

The detective wrote a lengthy note, then looked up at him. "As in, Damien-whose-last-name-she-doesn't-know? From the altercation at Bar Belles?"

"She knows my name. Now."

"And, despite her just learning your identity, you're here in the middle of the night?"

Damien's nostrils flared, and he struggled to bank his anger. Good thing he was a gargoyle and not a dragon, or he might well have puffed smoke or shot fire. "I don't like what you're implying, Detective."

"I'm not implying anything. I'm just trying to gather all the facts. At the bar, I got two conflicting stories. I was hoping to interview the Good Samaritan and get an accurate account of the event. Instead, I get a second call, supposedly involving the same two individuals, and I come to find out that not only does Miss Whitman know your name, you're spending the night with her. It doesn't take Sherlock Holmes to put all these clues together."

"Well, maybe that's who we need." Rina leapt to her feet and looked down on the detective. "You haven't given my story any credence since you first heard it. I don't care what clues you think you have, here are the facts."

She started ticking off items on her fingers as she lectured him. "One, Gretchen was attacked at the bar. I helped her get free. Two, I was then attacked. Damien—who was then a stranger—saved me. He left before you got there. Three, I was attacked again at work tonight. This time inside. Again by Dylan Ramer, only he had some of his goons with him. Our security staff stepped in. Thankfully, Damien also happened to be there. That's when I learned his name. Four, he was kind enough to see me home safely when my shift ended. He did *not* come upstairs with me. And who would have thought I'd be grateful for a broken window, because otherwise he wouldn't have heard me screaming, and I'd have been... violated. Or worse."

Rina plopped back down beside Damien and held her head in her hands.

He wanted so badly to comfort her, to hold her in his arms and tell her everything would be all right, but he couldn't. Not with Urbani watching. Not when he wasn't certain it would be okay.

Not if he couldn't control himself. Because if she was in his arms, he'd want to do a whole lot more than comfort her.

"Miss Whitman. For any injustices you've suffered, I deeply apologize. But you've made some strong allegations against Mr. Ramer. Allegations that he not only refutes, but ones that can ruin his life. Surely you understand we have to be thorough before we act. There is no room for error in this case."

Damien had spent enough time in the royal court when he was living to recognize veiled messages. "What about allegations that can ruin her reputation? What about protecting her life? And this case? What makes it so special? What aren't you telling us?"

"My job duties don't include telling persons of interest anything involving a case."

"Citizens who are attacked don't usually find themselves defending their actions. What's really going on here?"

Urbani turned around and addressed the officers who had accompanied him. "You gentlemen may leave. We're done here."

The officers filed out, and the detective followed them to the door.

Damien stood and followed him. "Detective?"

He stopped but didn't turn around.

"What makes this case so special?"

He glanced after the officers down the hall, turned toward Damien, then spoke in a low voice. "That's not the question you want to ask. What you really want to know is who would take an interest in the outcome of this case."

"Okay. Who would that be?"

"I've already said too much. Just think about it. Goodnight, Mr. Stone." He followed the officers down the hall.

Interesting. Who would be interested in the case? Had to be someone tying Urbani's hands. But how to find out?

"Damien?"

He turned toward Rina. Her eyes were large, her skin pale.

"Did you really hear me scream through the plastic over my window?"

"Yes. Of course." Did she know? Did she suspect? Surely not. How could she? "How else would I have heard you?"

"It's just..." She bit her lip, looked at the floor.

Fearful she'd discovered, or at least suspected, his secret—though how anyone would guess *that* he couldn't fathom—he tried to meet her gaze. But she wouldn't look at him. Damien put his finger under her chin then tipped up her head. "Talk to me."

"You got here so fast. It was like you just appeared out of thin air."

She was way off base. Relief washed over him, and he chuckled. "I assure you, I didn't. It felt like it took a lifetime. I wish I could have materialized out of thin air. Then I could have stopped him faster."

"I'm just glad you came at all. You saved me again." She wrapped her arms around him and pressed her head to his chest.

Could she feel his pulse quicken? His feelings for her were too raw, too huge. She represented his freedom, his life. But she'd pay too big a price for him. She deserved so much more than a warrior out of his realm, out of his time. What could he offer her? He didn't belong in her world.

Regardless, he couldn't leave her to fend off Ramer on her own. No warrior would leave anyone in jeopardy, and certainly not his beloved. His code of honor required him to protect her.

Damned if he stayed, damned if he left.

His thoughts turned to the portal to Hell, and he shivered.

Damned one way or another, so why not enjoy a few perks before eternal torment?

He rested his chin on the top of her head and breathed deeply. Even after a full night's work and another assault, she smelled fresh. Feminine. Alluring. He closed his eyes and tried to commit her to memory, to give him something to cling to when he... moved on. The appeal of her scent. The silkiness of her hair. The softness of her flesh.

Maybe that was hell. The everlasting realization that what you desired most was only a memory, its reality denied you forever.

She shifted in his arms and looked up at him. He gazed at her, fascinated by the freckles on her nose, the blush to her cheeks, the flecks of frost in her midnight blue eyes.

Unable to resist her any longer, he tipped his head down and brushed his lips softly against hers. He wanted to savor her, steep in her exquisite beauty, soar to the heavens on the sweetness of her kiss.

But she had different ideas.

This time it was she who deepened the kiss, she who grabbed his head and claimed his mouth for her own. She tasted of wine, rich and decadent, and he indulged his craving for her. He fisted her hair, held her head and body close to him, and feasted.

This memory alone could sustain him through all the torments of hell.

They were both breathless when the kiss ended. She looked up at him, a plea in her eyes, an invitation in her smile.

It would be so easy, so gratifying, to bed her. To learn every sensual curve, to bury himself so deeply in her that their souls fused as intimately as their bodies.

That would be a memory to last an eternity.

But it wouldn't be right to make promises with his body that his soul couldn't keep. He stepped back, steeled himself against the disappointment that flitted across her features, and turned their attentions to a romance-killing subject.

"Will you be safe here?"

"Are you asking me to come with you?"

Okay, so that backfired. It didn't squelch the mood like he thought it would, but rather gave her the opportunity to press her advantage.

"My day will be starting in less than an hour." It wasn't a lie. He could already feel the nearness of the dawn. Soon he'd have to make his way back to his plinth. Just another reason he couldn't lay with her. Just another reason she deserved so much more than he could offer.

She turned away and hugged herself. Was she cold, or seeking comfort? It didn't matter. He could do nothing for her in either regard. He had to take his leave.

"Do you work tomorrow? I'll try to stop by." He shouldn't. He should distance himself from her. Keep an eye on her from afar while letting her forget him.

"My shift starts at six. I'll look for you." She walked him to the door.

"Goodnight, Katarina."

Her breath caught when she heard her full name on his lips. He noted her eyelids flutter, her cheeks flush. Sorry for that and so many other things, he gave her a half-hearted smile then stepped into the hall.

"Damien?"

He turned, raised an eyebrow.

"How did you get in the building?"

His heart sank. He couldn't very well tell her he flew in her broken window. "I just opened the door. Must not have locked behind you." Yeah, like she'd believe that.

"But how did you know which apartment was mine?"

"You pointed out your unit while we stood outside. I knew which floor. After I got up here, I listened for a scuffle."

"It all happened so fast." Her voice trailed off, and she frowned.

"For me, it took an eternity to get to you. I feared I'd be too late. It's all in your perception, I guess."

"I guess." Her brow furrowed in thought.

He left before she could ask him anything else.

❖

Back on the roof of Nathaniel Burton Mansion, back in horned and winged form, Damien stretched, enjoying the mobility in his limbs before he petrified for the day.

"So, how'd it go?"

Damien jumped and almost fell off the roof. "Stop sneaking up on me, Anael."

"Sorry. I was just checking in."

"Sure you were. You know damn well how things are going. What do you really want?"

The angel put his hand on his chest and affected an expression of dramatic surprise. "You wound me, sir."

"Cut the crap. I'm almost out of time for the night."

Anael laughed and lost his theatrical demeanor. "You can always reach me." He tapped his temple. "Night or Day."

"Right. Last time I tried to communicate with you during the day, you ignored me."

"Well, I do have other duties to tend to."

"Sarcasm doesn't become you."

The angel shrugged.

"I don't know what you're playing at, but I'm out."

That got Anael's attention. He grabbed Damien by the shoulders and stared at him. "What do you mean, you're out?"

"Out. As in not in. I'm walking away. This thing between me and Rina can't work."

"You admit there is a thing."

Damien growled and started pacing. "It doesn't matter. We're too different. We're from different times and places. If I'd met her fifty, even one hundred years after I turned, it might be different. But now? There are vehicles and telephones and all manner of things that I've observed but never operated. I can't exist here as a human. If I tried, I'd only be a lodestone around her neck. I won't drag her down. She deserves so much more than I can give her."

"You don't know what you're talking about."

"I do. I can't provide for her. I'm not aware of any knights working in the Strip District. I can't meld seamlessly into her life. Can't share my history, introduce her to my family. It's all too complicated."

"You understand that you have entered your trial. If you fail at this, you don't just stay a protector."

"You mean a monster."

"I mean a gargoyle."

"I get it."

"Do you? Because you'll be in violation of the terms of your contract. You won't get into Heaven."

"Yeah, the vortex to hell. I know. Better I rot there than make Rina wither here."

"No, you don't know. It may take you eons to pass through the vortex, but pass you shall."

"You were serious about that? I thought the vortex was it."

Anael shook his head. "I don't lie, Damien."

"Okay, then. How much worse can it be?"

"Foolish boy." Anael clutched Damien's shoulder, then they both exploded into oblivion.

Damien's molecules scattered through dimensions he couldn't name, only to implode in on themselves in an agonizing assemblage of atoms. His head pounded, his stomach lurched, every cell in his body ignited in fiery torment. Damn that angel.

He gasped but only succeeded in inhaling thick embers. "I hate it when you do that to me, Anael. What the hell?"

"Not what, Damien," Anael said. "Where. It's against the rules, but you needed to see."

"Hell."

"The first level."

Damien choked on clouds of brimstone and looked around. Bodies hung on racks, some scourged by demonic creatures wielding whips of fire, others stretched until their limbs tore off only to reassemble and stretch again. Some souls were skinned and devoured, the torment cyclical, never-ending. Giant beasts with nine-inch claws and twelve-inch teeth tore people into bloody shreds. They gnawed on the bones of writhing beings, snarling and snapping at anything near them.

There was no blessed retreat into unconsciousness or death. This was their other side, their ever-after, their eternity. The tormented endured each torture, alert and unprotected. Impossibly hot gusts of wind howled through the cavern, tossing unmanacled departed souls from one horror to the next. And the maniacal screeches of the tormentors were only overpowered by the anguished wails of the damned.

"I've seen enough." Damien's words were barely intelligible through his coughing and wheezing.

"Are you certain? This is only the first level. The second level hosts souls feeding on their own entrails, or having a myriad of sadistic violations forced upon them. Rape. Sodomy. Bestiality. Then there's—"

Damien clutched Anael's arm. "Enough!"

"Do you understand now?"

Damien looked up and howled, his throat burning, his voice mingling into the sounds of all the other lost souls, an agonizing dirge melodic only to Satan himself.

When he thought the devil's name, the most sinister laugh echoed through the cavern, a shadow given voice and power. It sent chills down his burning spine. The demons cheered, their victims cowered, and Damien cringed, seeking escape that would only be denied him.

The angel shook Damien's shoulder. "Stop making me do this. Tell me you understand now."

Damien collapsed to the ground, his skin melting and fusing to the burning rock below him. He opened his mouth to scream, but his lungs burned too much to muster a sound.

"Tell me, Damien!" The angel had to scream over the uproar in the cavern.

Damien barely heard him, hardly registered meaning to the words. All was misery. All was despair. All was lost.

Anael gripped his shoulder. Again he exploded into nothingness.

Eight

Rina stared at the newly taped down plastic over her window. Right outside that flimsy film was her fire escape. Between its proximity to her broken window and the way the last bit of film had been pulled away from the frame, she had to assume that was how Ramer got in.

Bad enough he knew where she lived. He basically had an open invitation.

No way would she sleep tonight.

She clutched the empty wine bottle like a weapon and stared at the window. If anyone even tried to enter, she'd clobber them.

A shift and a slouch, and she was in a more comfortable position, alert and ready for what the early morning hours would bring. Then her thoughts took off.

She still couldn't understand how Damien had gotten in. Would have made much more sense if he had gotten in that way, too. But somehow reaching the bottommost ladder of the fire escape without a partner would have taken time.

No, he had to have come in the front door and run up the stairs. But how? That door was locked. Maybe it really didn't close tightly behind her when she entered.

That would be a first. That door slammed shut on its own, often before she was ready. More times than she could count, she'd had to dig out her keys again with arms full of groceries or mail. Or gotten bruises on her arm or nearly lost a finger trying to hold it open.

The only way Damien could have known he'd get in would have been through the window.

But unless he had a ten-foot vertical jump, he'd never have reached the ladder to pull it down.

Besides, instinct would have sent him to the door. Maybe adrenaline forced the door open, like mothers lifting cars off their babies.

Humph. Not likely.

Which took her back to the window. Which was impossible. It wasn't like he could fly.

She got a flash of a vision, something she couldn't quite snatch from her memory and make clear. Something about flying?

Her eyes snapped open, her heart skipped a beat.

Wings.

She swore she saw wings the first time they kissed. But people didn't have wings. *Damien* didn't have wings. He was a warm-blooded man. Hot-blooded. All man.

Unless...

She thought about his hesitance to be with her, and about how his kisses made her feel. Floating. Soaring. Transcended.

Could it be? Was Damien... an angel?

Rina tried to process that latest thought, but her eyelids grew heavy.

Then they snapped open.

His wings didn't have feathers.

Rina laughed at her revelation. People don't have wings. Period. But—

Impossible.

She yawned, fought against the exhaustion. Closed her eyes again.

What if—she yawned again—someone broke in?

No answer manifested before she fell into a deep sleep.

Rina blinked and looked around. The blanket of fog rolling in from the river gave her the first of many clues that she'd somehow left the relative safety of her apartment. For starters, there was fog. And the river.

All that aside, the music was what really gave it away. It wasn't classical. Not really. Nor symphonic, nor operatic. It defied description. She'd never heard anything so glorious before. The melody seemed to flow in her blood, the harmony tingled her senses.

This was why ballerinas danced, tenors sang, musicians played. Why poets and composers wrote. Why artists sculpted, painted, or sketched. Why couples married and babies warmed the hearts of even the coldest souls.

This was the answer to every important 'why' ever asked.

She didn't mind not being in her apartment. Didn't care if she ever left wherever she was. All that mattered was the feeling of completeness, of compassion. Of love.

A misty figure formed in the fog, took shape, then floated to her through the nebulous vapor. She averted her eyes when he reached her, his radiance too bright for her unworthy eyes. But she was compelled to look at him. His countenance glowed brighter than sunlight reflecting off the purest snow-bank, his visage fierce yet friendly, powerful yet protective. Taller than the mighty sequoia, vast as the ocean is deep. Yet intimate, familiar.

Familiar.

She peeked at him again, squinted into the glare. Unable to stand the brightness, she looked away, but something about him tickled her memory. He looked like someone she knew. That person's identity eluded her, as did the reason for this man's appearance. But she didn't care. She floated along to the fantasia and basked in the joy of the moment.

"Katarina." His voice, a baritone timbre, seemed to rise and fall with the melody, blending into the strains as though his words were part of the song.

"Do I know you?"

"Who I am is immaterial. I come to herald glad tidings and impart an important message."

Still unable to do anything other than squint at him, she looked around. Three rivers burbled and flowed past the fountain at the Point, the light—not sunlight, but something else, something more—reflected off white ripples in the water, cast rainbow-colored holograms in the spray. The city's buildings rose like spires into lofty clouds above. Definitely Pittsburgh, yet definitely not. No traffic, no gridlock, no noise.

Was she in an alternate reality? A parallel universe?

"No, my dear Katarina."

Her eyes snapped open. Had she spoken her musings aloud?

"No. You didn't speak, and we aren't elsewhere. We're in your imagination. And yet not. We're... well, where we are is of no consequence. It's the *why* that matters."

"Because of your glad tidings and whatnot?"

"Ah, the whatnot is of great import."

"I'm confused." Rina held her hand to her eyes against the glare and tried to focus on him. She knew him. Or someone similar to him. If she could just place who, this might make more sense.

"Stop trying to identify me. Instead, know this. You have doubts."

"About you? About where we are and what you want?"

He sighed. "No. About Damien."

"What do you know about Damien?"

"We really have no time for this. About your questions—"

"I have a ton of them."

"I'm not here to answer them. I'm here to tell you not to seek the answers. Just accept these three fundamental truths. One, Damien means you no harm. Two, you need him. And three, he needs you. Nothing else matters."

Despite the peace flowing through her, she couldn't accept his words. She grew less compliant, less in tune with her surroundings. Discomfort ached in her bones, in her veins, but she had too many questions to blindly accept this man's message.

She shook her head. "No. The answers do matter. I don't understand."

"Take it on faith."

"That isn't enough."

He shook his head. Turned away and muttered, "Wish they were all as amenable as Mary."

"Mary? Who's Mary? Is she why Damien is being so secretive?"

"You are strong-willed."

He seemed to deflate, his radiance dimmed. She made out more of his features. The strong physique, the golden hair. The amber eyes.

Al DeAngelo? Damien's friend? But, why? How? What—?

Again, he sighed. "Too inquisitive. Too strong-willed."

"Al?"

He pointed at her forehead. "You will forget all about this dream, forget everything but my message. Sleep soundly, and when you rise, feel these truths. Take them to heart, and heed my advice."

"But—"

Al touched her brow, then she sank into deepest slumber.

Nine

Damien hadn't just spent the day in his stone prison. He spent it unconscious, recovering. When the sun set, his body began the transformation process, triggering him to wake.

His nightmare flooded back to him.

The smoke. The ash. The torment and the agony. The despair.

The eternal futility of it all.

But it wasn't a nightmare, was it? Not really. Anael had broken the rules for him. Again. Because Damien was frustrated and agitated—and, if he had to admit it, scared—Anael had gone against his mandates, first taking him to the vortex and then, last night, into hell itself.

Well, the first level of hell. He shrugged off a shudder when he considered what the other levels might entail.

God, he didn't want to end up there. He wanted to keep Rina safe. But given their differences, he still believed the best thing for her would be for him to keep his distance. Protect her from afar. He had thought it would result in eternal punishment, and he'd accepted it. Had been willing to suffer the torments of the vortex in order to let her live a free and full life.

But hell? The different levels of hell?

He shivered. Despite his instincts to protect Rina—instincts that indicated he should stay away—he couldn't. It wasn't his body's desire for her, although that was ridiculously difficult to deny. It wasn't even his dormant noble sense of chivalry.

No. It was his fear. Fear of eternal damnation. Fear of burning and rotting and being eaten alive.

In level one. What if he was sent deeper?

Clearly he wasn't the brave and noble warrior he once was, and maybe he never had been. Did that matter?

Of course it did. Because if he didn't even have honor and bravery left in him, he truly had nothing to offer Rina.

That thought chilled even his monstrous form. Made him consider abandoning his bargain and suffering hell just to protect her.

Foolish. That was the kind of thinking that made Anael break the rules for him. Twice.

And he couldn't help but wonder what the penalty was for that.

"Anael?"

He waited for the angel to appear. Wanted to apologize, wanted to discuss a possible counter agreement.

But the angel didn't show. Didn't answer.

"Anael?"

Still he waited, and still no sign of the angel.

He had said he always heard Damien. Heard when he spoke aloud, heard when he tried to hide errant thoughts.

So where was he?

Dear God. Was the angel punished? Banished? Worse?

For breaking one small rule—albeit twice—because of him.

Damien scratched between his horns and considered doing something he hadn't done in centuries. He called for the angel one last time, and when he didn't answer, Damien bowed his head.

And prayed.

"Lord. My humblest apologies. I don't know if You're willing to listen to the prayers of a man who hasn't spoken to You in years, but if You are so inclined to give me Your mercy and Your attention, I have yet another favor to ask."

Another favor. The last time he begged God for something, he lay bleeding on the battlefield, pleading for another chance at life. His wish had been granted, but not like he had hoped. Anael told him the gargoyle deal was a blessing, but it felt like a curse. It had been so long. Would God even listen this time, and if so, how would He grant this wish?

"Lord, I didn't realize when I asked Your first favor what the terms truly entailed. Please allow me to pass on as I should have centuries ago, without fulfilling the terms of the contract."

Damien waited for some kind of sign. When he made the first bargain, there had been bright light, fanfare, an army of angels. Anael, contract in hand.

This time, the night remained dark, silent. Lonely. And no Anael.

Where was that angel?

"Lord?" Dare he ask anything else? Given his latest request went unanswered, was he due to have his next wish granted? Or had he already exceeded his limit?

It couldn't hurt to ask another favor. Not one so important. "If You won't renegotiate with me, please spare Anael whatever punishment he's suffering. He may have broken a rule, but it was for my benefit."

Still nothing.

Maybe he would have felt more in tune with God now if

he had been praying for the last several hundred years. What a foul-weather worshipper he was. No wonder God didn't answer him this time.

Still, poor Anael. Punished. All because—

"Damien?"

Damien jumped at the sound of Anael's voice. He spun around to find the angel standing there. He didn't float, he didn't glow. Didn't even smile like he usually did.

But he was there.

"Are you all right?" Damien asked. "I've been worried."

"You didn't make me break the rules, Damien. I chose to."

"Because I was being stubborn."

"It doesn't matter. It was my choice."

"I didn't think angels had freewill."

"How do you think we got the fallen? Sometimes we're left to our own devices. And sometimes, we choose wrong."

Damien tried and failed to shrug off the chills creeping up his spine. When he spoke, his voice croaked, barely above a whisper. "Did I make you... fall?"

"Stop worrying about me."

"I'm sorry." He was. Profoundly so.

Anael turned away from Damien and walked to the edge of the roof. He looked out over the lights of the city, didn't turn around when he spoke.

"Damien. You need to forget about new terms to your contract. Operate as though nothing has changed."

"If I'm not getting to renegotiate, then nothing has changed."

Anael didn't turn around.

"Anael? Has something changed?"

"Claim your destiny, Damien. Allow me to worry about mine."

With that, the angel disappeared.

Damien called out to him, but he never returned.

A quick roll of his head released the tension in his neck. For about two seconds. Then the stress settled back on him, heavier than the stone of his alter ego.

Anael was in trouble. Because of him.

The terms of his deal were absolute—claim his destined future or forfeit his eternity.

Without the angel, without new terms, he had no choice.

Stretching his wings, he took to the sky.

He needed to find Rina.

Damien perched on the roof across from Bar Belles. He kept one eye out for Anael and the other for Dylan Ramer.

Neither showed.

When the last patron filtered out of the bar, he soared down to street level, transformed into a true human form—it was getting easier and easier to do that—then leaned against a lamppost, waiting for Rina to leave.

She walked out with Gretchen and Tiny, stopped short when she saw him standing there.

"When you didn't come in, I didn't know if I would see you again."

Tiny crossed his arms and glared at him. Gretchen also sent him a dirty look.

"I didn't want to bother you while you were on duty. Figured I'd just wait out here until you left."

"Anything noteworthy going on?" Tiny asked.

Must have assumed he'd been keeping an eye out for Ramer. The bouncer wasn't wrong. He had looked for the scumbag, but the guy never showed. Didn't know if that was a good thing or a bad thing.

Damien shook his head. "No. Been quiet."

The frost in Gretchen's eyes warmed a bit, and she

waggled her eyebrows. Then she linked her arm through Tiny's. "Let's go. I'm sure Damien can see Rina home safely."

Tiny smiled. They both said goodnight then headed up the street.

Rina sighed. "I'm sorry. You don't have to walk me home. I can get there myself."

"Not going to happen."

"I could call a cab."

"I can see you home."

"Are you sure? I mean, you didn't come in tonight, and—"

"That's because I was out here. Like I said, I didn't want to bother you."

"Well, I have a lot of energy to burn. I'm not really tired."

"We can go somewhere first." He patted his pocket, felt the wallet there. Hopefully, if the billfold was there, the money would be too. Another rule Anael broke for him. "You hungry?"

She shook her head. "I think I'd really just like to walk."

He offered her his elbow. "Lead the way."

Rina slipped her arm in his, then they headed up the street at a brisk clip.

"You are full of energy tonight."

"I slept in. Lately I've been an insomniac, but last night, I slept like I was drugged. Had the strangest dream. When I finally woke up, I felt so fresh and invigorated. The energy still hasn't worn off."

"So I see."

She slowed. "I'm sorry. Am I walking too fast for you."

A smile crossed his face. "No. I'm just surprised someone with short legs can cover so much ground so fast."

"Short legs!" She stopped walking and looked down.

He couldn't help it. He looked at her legs, too. Her toned, shapely legs. Legs he knew from experience to be silky and soft.

Legs he wanted wrapped around him. Or spread before him.

He looked up to find her staring at him. Ashamed she'd caught him looking—and had probably guessed what he'd been thinking—he felt grateful she couldn't make out the flush of his cheeks in the dark of the night. A quick clear of his throat, then he answered as glibly as he could manage. "Well, shorter than mine."

The crack in his voice meant he didn't quite pull off the innocent act.

She smiled and resumed her fast pace. "Nice save, Damien."

It wasn't. But he appreciated her letting it go.

"I changed my mind. I am hungry. Care to get something to eat?"

For her, anything. "I'm up for a snack if you are. Lead the way."

She led them toward the university district to an eatery famous for fries and hotdogs. They agreed to split a large order of fries with cheese and gravy. She ordered a vanilla milkshake, and he ordered a beer. He had no idea there were so many kinds. The cashier grew frustrated while he scanned the names of hundreds, so he just chose one at random.

Rina ordered a hotdog with mustard, hold the onions, and looked at him.

He declined anything else to eat. His appetite was pretty much nonexistent at that point, anyway. He wasn't used to eating. Wasn't even sure if he could. But if he was truly in human form, maybe he could. Maybe he needed to.

All that thinking made his head hurt. He pushed his concerns aside and took out his wallet. Nerves churned acid in his stomach until he opened it and saw that he did indeed still have money. He counted out the bills Anael had provided him until he had enough to cover their check then led her to the main dining area. A few pub crawlers were scattered throughout, most near the walls, so he headed for a section near the windows, hoping for a little privacy.

Rina frowned the whole way to their table.

After they sat, he took her hand and squeezed it. She didn't return the motion.

"What's the matter?"

She pulled her hand away and looked out the window. "You said you were hungry, but you didn't order anything. But I did. Then you paid. I'm not a charity case."

He didn't understand things in this world. Weren't men supposed to provide? He realized she earned her own living, but if he was able to pay for her, shouldn't he?

Who was he kidding? He couldn't provide anything. The money wasn't his. Not really.

He chose his words carefully. "I don't think of you as a charity case."

"Then why did you pay when I ordered more? Why did you agree to come out with me if you weren't even hungry? Why did you even want to walk me home?"

"Why? Because I wanted to. I wanted to be certain you were safe."

She continued to frown.

The waitress approached. She put the food on the table between them, looked at Rina's expression, and made a hasty retreat.

He cleared his throat, uncomfortable with the situation. "And... I wanted to be with you."

Rina's icy expression melted, and she smiled at him. "Really?"

"Of course."

She reached across the table, squeezed his hand, then started eating.

Throat dry, he drained half his beer—so unlike the ale he'd had in Europe, yet the most delicious thing he could fathom. He swallowed the brew and watched her. Okay, maybe he could think of one thing that looked more appetizing. She even ate with delicate purpose, taking tiny nibbles and not getting any toppings on her face or fingers.

How could he not want her? Or want to protect her? She was precious. Priceless.

Looking at her was almost painful, so he glanced down at the plate of fries. He'd never seen so many potatoes piled onto one plate. His stomach soured, flopped.

What the hell was wrong with him? He hadn't had the opportunity to eat human food in centuries. And instead of savoring it, he was sickened by it.

Okay, if he was honest, it wasn't the food that disturbed him. It was wondering about what came next.

Rina wiped her fingers and mouth with a paper napkin and looked at him over the mountain of food. "You aren't eating."

"I'm just not in the mood, I guess."

She stood up and extended her hand toward him. When he took it, she pulled him to his feet. "Maybe we can find something else you're in the mood for, then."

They left the eatery and began strolling toward her building.

With another abrupt stop, she turned and looked at him. "You know, I thought a walk in the park might be nice."

"In the middle of the night?" Was she insane? Or just foolhardy?

"Don't lecture me."

He swallowed a sigh. "Okay."

"I thought maybe the fresh air would do me some good. But I don't really want to go there."

He shrugged. "Then where to? I'm up for anything."

"Good." She started walking again, this time much faster than her earlier pace. "I hope you mean that. Because we're going back to my place."

Damien's emotions waged a violent war while he and Rina raced to her apartment. His need to protect her made him want to keep his distance. Fear for his immortal soul made him accept her invitation. Which, to be honest, wasn't much of a hardship. Because desire for her flooded through him, and his body definitely sided with that emotion.

Then came the guilt. If he slept with her, he would be using her to stay out of hell. He had a code of honor. Or at least, he used to. No matter. He didn't use women. Not like that. Women were a source of pleasure, or maybe sometimes nothing more than a necessary physical release. But he never took one without her consent, and never did so with an ulterior motive.

Rina might be consenting, but she had no idea what his motives were. And she wouldn't consent if she did.

Which brought shame into the fight.

And embarrassment wasn't far behind. His motives were shameful. Not to mention it had been centuries since he'd lain with a woman. Had the act changed? Did women expect something different? Would he be able to satisfy her? Worse, would he be able to control himself before ravaging her? He just wasn't sure what she expected. Or what he would bring to their coupling.

What was the modern expression? It was like riding a bike. Well, he'd never ridden a bike, so that analogy did him no good.

His feelings caromed through him, one after another, battling for supremacy.

All too soon, they reached her apartment. When Rina ran up the stairs with Damien in tow, he still didn't know which emotion would win.

She opened the door, pulled him inside, slammed him

against the wall. Then she claimed his mouth in a passionate kiss.

Just like that, all the soldiers fell. All, that is, but desire, who leveled the battlefield with blazing speed. Hail, hail, the conquering hero.

And conquer, he did.

Ten

When Rina woke, she shivered. Goosebumps spread over her flesh, and the sheets were cool when she reached across the bed.

Damien had gone.

Bolting upright, she clutched the sheet to her chest, blinked to clear her vision, and squinted to see in the dark. No hulking figure sat in her chair, no massive body stood in her doorway.

Alone. He'd left her alone.

She wrapped herself in her blanket then padded out to the living room. Damien had turned on a table lamp, and a warm glow bathed the room. The empty room.

A sigh escaped her. Came from deep inside her and whooshed out in a slow, steady stream of dejection. Working at Bar Belles had taught her—and taught her fast—that men often used women for a quick fling and then didn't return. Not until they needed another release. She swore she'd never be one of those women. Certainly not professionally, like the dancers at the club. But also not personally. She vowed she'd only be with a man if they had an emotional connection, a potential future.

Did he deceive her, or did her desires overrule her better judgment? She wanted to blame him, wanted to rail at the unfairness of it all. But she crumpled to the sofa, bereft. She had no one to blame but herself. She'd invited him to her apartment. She'd invited him to her bed.

But she'd never asked his intentions.

Pain sliced through her, a poisoned lance straight to the heart, its toxin spreading through her as fast and far as Damien had caused pleasure to consume her the night before. A tear rolled down her cheek, then another, and another. Soon she shook with gut-wracking sobs, waited to die from the shame and the hurt and the betrayal.

But she wouldn't be so lucky. She'd live. Well, she'd survive.

Would she? What if he made a habit of bedding women and then leaving? How many women had there been? Why had she lost all control and not insisted on a condom? Sure, she was protected against pregnancy, but the pill wouldn't protect her from all the skanks he'd slept with. From any disease he may have given her.

Not only had she risked her heart, she'd risked her life. A gamble not worth the stakes. Especially since she was already dealt such a shitty hand.

No. No more crying. She swiped the tears off her face with the back of her hand, then she leaned over to switch off the light. Something white caught her eye. She looked closer. A piece of paper was tucked under the base of the lamp.

Rina sighed, but she picked up the paper. Holding it under the lampshade, she looked at the nearly illegible scrawl.

I have no token to leave as a thank you, so I offer you this drawing as a symbol of my affection.

~Damien

In the bottom right corner, he'd drawn a crude representation of a rose.

Her heart swelled at the sweet gesture, and she hugged the note to her chest.

But then all her insecurities came rushing back.

He hadn't stayed. Hadn't mentioned getting together again. Hadn't even had the courage to say goodbye in person. No. All he'd left was a token of his thanks.

None of that boded well for a future together. Nor did it erase her fears from not having used a condom.

She closed her eyes and groaned.

What the hell had she been thinking?

Rina switched off the light then curled into a fetal position on the sofa, wrapped in her blanket. The room wasn't as dark as she expected, and she looked at the digital clock on her cable box. It was nearly dawn.

A shadow darkened the room, and she looked at the window. She thought she saw a figure outside, but the fire escape was at her bedroom window, not in her living room. No one could have been there, hovering five stories above the ground. She shook her head at her silly thoughts.

Then she swore she heard a strange howl carry on the wind.

Rina scoffed. No wild animals lived in the city.

The first sun's rays peeked in her window, brightening her room.

Too bad it couldn't brighten her mood. She hadn't felt such gloom in years.

Eleven

Damien barely made it to his plinth before he petrified into stone. As it was, he'd be balancing in a precarious position all day, and assuming he didn't tumble to the sidewalk below and shatter into rubble, he'd rise that evening sore and cramped.

Every twinge of pain would be so worth it. Even if he tumbled to the ground and broke into dust, he'd go to his end a happy man. Wonder if any gargoyle had ever been carved with so ridiculous a grin on its face?

Then guilt consumed him, the maniacal smile frozen on his face no match for the cold shame that settled over him.

If he could frown in his stone state, he would.

He wasn't a man. Not really.

Remorse enveloped him, settled dark in his heart even as the sun brightened his form.

He'd used her.

It wasn't that he didn't have feelings for her. No, far from it. But being with her kept him from eternal damnation, which made her a tool. As he had nothing to offer her, other than his company, he was sickened by how quickly he'd abandoned his code of honor.

It wasn't fair to her. Wasn't right.

He hadn't even been able to hold her until she woke, feel her soft, pliant flesh pressed against him, head to toe, warming under his rough palms as he caressed her skin. Couldn't watch the sun's rays creep into her room and shine on her riotous curls, highlighting their flaxen beauty, before landing on her luminous skin, skimming over her face until her eyes fluttered open. Couldn't relish in that first smile of the day, a smile reserved for remembering dreams and greeting lovers.

Couldn't even enjoy a cup of coffee or a crumb of bread together.

Oh, but the moments he had been able to hold her? Perfection. He couldn't imagine eternity in Heaven being any more glorious.

He basked in the memories of their night together, reveled in the pleasure he'd given and received.

Then felt all the more guilty for enjoying those memories, those moments, with her.

While his emotions continued to spin out of control, Anael appeared beside him.

If he'd been able to react, he'd have jumped. And probably fallen to his destruction. Instead, he thought a string of curse words at the angel.

Anael clucked his tongue, then began a conversation with Damien inside his mind.

"So, you decided to embrace your destiny."

"I don't know about that."

"You spent the night with her."

"Damn it, Anael. You're in my head. You know what I'm thinking. Don't make me say the words aloud."

"Well, technically, you aren't speaking at the moment."

Damien thought another litany of curses.

The angel floated to the other side of Damien. Because of the contorted way he'd petrified on the plinth, his range of vision was limited. Anael was out of his line of sight.

"You aren't using her, Damien."

"Could have fooled me. What's she get out of the deal? A guy who can barely function in this era. A man with no job, no family, no home." No honor.

"Fool. Of course you have honor. The rest doesn't matter."

"I didn't say that, er, think that to you."

"I'm in your head, remember? Doesn't matter what thoughts are meant for me. I can hear them all."

"Well, stop eavesdropping."

"I don't have a choice. You aren't very forthcoming with your feelings when you're animated. But inanimate? Why, it's almost like you're made of stone. Completely silent."

"You're not funny."

"I amuse myself."

"That makes one of us."

Anael floated back into Damien's view. "In all seriousness—"

"Who was laughing?"

"We have a problem. Well, a couple of problems, actually. Technically, three."

Damien knew his body was solid stone, but he swore his pulse quickened. Fluttered just for a beat. Was Rina in danger? How could he help her? He paused, would have closed his eyes and taken a deep breath if his lungs worked. "Just get on with it."

"First, Dylan Ramer is using his connections to put the heat on Katarina."

"What connections? What's he up to?" His heart definitely raced inside his stone body. He knew, because his pulse thundered in his sculpted ears, pounded in his solid chest. "Can you get me to her? Or help her yourself? Do something, Anael!"

"Don't worry. She's not in immediate danger. We have time."

Another pause when he would have struggled to catch his breath and settle his nerves. "That detective alluded to Ramer having connections. What do you know? Give me the details."

"That takes me to problem number two. I'm no longer allowed to intervene."

"You never were allowed."

"True. Yet I took you to the vortex. I took you to the first level. I nudged you in Katarina's direction. Talked to her to help you along." His voice grew softer. "Appeared to her in a dream."

"You did *what?*"

"Like I said, or tried to, I've been breaking too many rules. My wings are metaphorically clipped. I've probably said too much to you now." He looked up at the sky as though he waited for something to fall on him. Or snatch him from where he floated.

"What were you doing in her dreams?"

"Helping you."

"You crossed a line, Anael."

"Yes, well, apparently you aren't the only one who feels that way."

"Is that why she was with me last night? Did you manipulate her?" He should have known. No way would a woman of her worth want someone like him.

"Stop the mental flagellation. I didn't coerce her. She wants you."

"Stay away from her, angel. She's off limits."

"Not a problem. As I've mentioned, I've been ordered to stand down."

Small comfort. "What's the third problem?"

The angel sighed, buffed his nails on his tunic.

"Anael?"

"Because of my... let's call it interference, shall we? Because of my interference, another player has been put into the game."

"You mean, you aren't my handler anymore?"

"No, you're still my charge. At least, for now."

"Then what are you talking about?"

He looked up at the sky again. "They feel I've tipped the scales too far. They've introduced another to balance things, tip them back a bit."

"They? Who's they? I thought this deal was with God. And what do you mean, tipped the scales? All you've done is nag and embarrass me and intrude on Katarina's subconscious mind."

"Now someone has been dispatched to even things out."

"Who?"

"I can't say."

"Can't? Or won't?"

"Does it matter?"

Damien thought about it. "I guess not. But some information might be nice."

"That's what got us in trouble in the first place!" The angel swelled, glowed, and disappeared. Then he rematerialized. "I'm sorry. I believe I've been on this world too long. I've developed some nasty traits. Anger. Frustration. Hubris."

"Did you happen to develop pity or compassion? Maybe an insuppressible desire to share information?"

Anael closed his eyes, took a deep breath. "I used to be patient. Used to follow the rules without question. You've been a negative influence on me, Damien. With your petulant whining, continuous doubt, and constant foul mood. Whether I have compassion or pity is not the point. I've intervened enough, some think too much. Know that Katarina is about to have trouble. You are about to have troubles of your own. And I can't help you. Either of you."

Anael vanished before Damien could reply.

⁜

Damien didn't know how long he reached his thoughts out to Anael. It didn't matter. The angel didn't reappear, didn't answer.

Things were bad enough when he had to decide between her happy mortal life and his damned eternal soul. Despite an all-consuming desire to protect her, he'd been selfish. He'd chosen his salvation and brought her into his life, such as it was.

The consequence? He'd opened her world to untold troubles and dangers.

He should have just protected her from afar, kept his distance and kept her safe.

But no, he listened to Anael, got his hopes up. Entertained the thought that maybe he could have it all.

He'd had centuries to learn better. Hundreds of years to grow accustomed to his existence. And thousands of days to regret making his deal.

If he had known then that he'd have spent millions of moments, one exactly like another, still as stone, growing more and more cynical, losing more and more of the honorable man he'd once been—well, had he known, he would have accepted his impending death. Not happily, but he'd have embraced it with a knight's honor and determination.

Instead, he'd been weak. Scared. Unready to leave the world, unprepared to breech eternity.

Little did he know he'd be stuck in purgatory until now.

By the time he'd found his salvation, he had no way of claiming it without tainting its beauty.

Oh, Katarina. What he wouldn't give to have met her in his own time. Or to fit into hers.

But that was just it, wasn't it? He had nothing to give. Only guilt. A lifetime of hiding, explaining. Lying and struggling.

He'd been weak centuries ago, fearing the unknown. And

he'd been weak again the night before, bedding Rina and considering a future with her.

His weakness brought danger to her door. Anael wouldn't tell him who or what was coming, but if it was to balance the cosmic scales, it had to be formidable.

Was he strong enough to protect her from it? To defeat it and banish it so Rina would be safe?

His only choice was to do what he'd been afraid of so long ago. Accept his destiny and leave this world.

But first, he'd make certain she was protected. He'd just have to do it from a distance.

Twelve

Rina blew off all her commitments that day in favor of wallowing in self-pity and watching rom-coms on cable. She had all day and all night to cry into her coffee. Or beer. It was her night off, and she only had one class that morning. Which she had no intention of dragging her sorry ass to.

Didn't even suffer any guilt about blowing off classes. She had straight A's, anyway. Missing a class or two wouldn't be detrimental to her GPA. Besides, she was considering changing majors. Other than teaching, she didn't know what she'd do with a degree in European History.

By the fifth happily-ever-after ending, she wanted to throw something at her television.

Then she remembered her window. Repairing it was a necessary task she kept postponing.

Hell with it. The super could deal with it. She'd pay the up-charge.

So what if Ramer got in her apartment again? She didn't plan on being there. Time to get her life in order. She'd clean herself up, pack her things, and move on to bigger and better.

She took a long, hot bath, luxuriating in the lavender scent of the bubbles. She imagined living in a tiny cottage in the countryside in Europe, growing vegetables in her backyard garden, sipping wine and nibbling cheese that her lover had brought home from the village. He was a tall man—strong, silent—with dark, close-cropped hair and mysterious gray eyes.

He'd reach for her, sweep some loose curls from her face, trail his work-roughened fingers along her jawline. A soft kiss on her forehead, a lingering one on her lips, then he'd slant his mouth over hers.

She'd wrap her arms around him, cling to him so she didn't collapse at his feet. His knight's armor was hard and cold under her—

Knight's armor? What the hell?

She blinked to clear her vision, tried to rectify her European dream with her Pittsburgh bathroom. Water and suds had sloshed over the tub's edge, pooling on the tile. Hopefully no water had leaked through to her neighbor's ceiling below.

The daydream left her confused. She wanted to forget all about it and get out of the tub, but once again, the image of her brave knight came to her. Overwhelmed her.

Damien.

With his face foremost in her thoughts, she sobbed.

That was the only way she'd ever get to be with him again —in her dreams and fantasies. A poor imitation of the real thing that left her empty. And alone.

Rina waved to her friend and beckoned her to the booth she'd chosen in the back of the diner. Then she smiled her thanks at the waitress who placed her drink and nachos order on the table in front of her.

"Can I please get an unsweet tea? Thanks." Gretchen slid

into the seat opposite Rina when the server walked away. "Sorry I'm late."

"Couldn't find a place to park?"

"Had to walk. I still haven't saved enough to get my car out of impound." She plucked a loaded chip out of her friend's dish then popped it into her mouth.

"Want a nacho?"

"Touchy. I figured you got that so we could share."

Rina pushed the plate to the center of the table. "I don't mind. And I'm sorry. I guess I am a little grumpy today."

"What gives?" She grabbed another chip, scraped it over the guacamole piled on top of the nachos, then ate the whole thing in one bite. The waitress brought her drink, and she took a generous sip before putting the glass down and staring at her friend. "Since I quit smoking, I've had a big-ass case of the munchies."

"You haven't cheated?"

"Nope. Not a single cigarette since the last one you saw me smoke. A bunch of nicotine gum, though. And patches. So many I think I'm getting a rash." She scratched at her arm.

"You need to take better care of yourself. And stop snacking so much. You don't want to get fat." She pulled the dish back toward her.

Gretchen held her hands up. "Keep your chips."

Rina sighed.

"Seriously, Ri. What's up?"

"I'm leaving."

"Because I took a couple of chips?" She reached into her purse. "I'll pay you for the damn things."

"No. Don't be ridiculous. I don't mean I'm leaving the restaurant. I mean I'm leaving Pittsburgh."

"What?" Gretchen nearly knocked her glass over in her haste to grab her friend's hand. "What are you talking about? What's going on? Why?"

"Slow down. I didn't just bail on you and skip town. I'm here to say goodbye."

"No. No goodbyes."

"Gretchen, you're the only thing keeping me here. I'll keep in touch. I promise. But I have nothing left here, and I need to go."

"Bullshit. I want to know what has you on the run. Is it Ramer?"

She shrugged. "He's part of it, I guess. I just need a change."

"Updating your wardrobe is a change. Straightening your hair. Dying it brown. Or blue. Moving isn't a change. It's a retreat. A surrender. You're running from something, and that's not like you. You're a stay-and-fight kind of girl."

"I'm not retreating. I'm exploring new options."

"You're almost done with school. After graduation, you'll get a real job, then you can explore all kinds of new options."

"A real job?" She scoffed. "Have you looked on the career boards lately? How many 'Wanted—History Major with No Measurable Life Skills' jobs have you seen?"

"Don't you think maybe you should have considered that before you majored in it?"

Rina sighed and took a sip of her own drink.

"You could try law school. We could do it together. It would be fun!"

It was a good thing looks couldn't kill because she'd have missed Gretchen.

"Okay. Dial the rage back a bit. I know you don't want to spend more money on grad school. And we both know you'd die a slow death studying law."

"I can't imagine why, seeing as it's been so helpful to me thus far."

Gretchen snatched another loaded chip. "Urbani isn't the problem."

Rina's eyebrows shot up. "Really? He just gets a pass?"

"Not a pass, but—You know what? It doesn't matter. I don't believe for one second this is about the detective, school, or your poor career options."

"I don't want to be stuck at Bar Belles my whole life."

"No one does. But that's no different than yesterday. Tell me what this is really about."

Rina thought about taking a big bite of nachos to avoid speaking the truth, but the thought of eating anything at the moment made her stomach lurch. Besides, she'd asked Gretchen there not just to say goodbye, but to get some advice.

"I slept with Damien."

"What?"

She told Gretchen the whole story, leaving out only her unbridled fantasies.

"He was gone before dawn? What'd you do all day?"

"Watched pathetic rom-coms and took stock of my life. I can't stay here, Gretch. Not when I know I might bump into him at any time. Not when I have to wonder if I'll see him at the club, or see him with another woman. I just can't."

"I've never seen your knickers so twisted over a guy before."

"Don't you get it? He made me break my one hard-and-fast rule."

"What was the problem? Not hard enough? Or too fast?"

She snatched a cheesy chip off the plate and threw it toward her friend. It landed with a plop on the table.

Gretchen swiped it into a napkin and wiped up the mess. "I was just joking."

Rina glared at her.

"You mean the so-selective-you-never-have-sex rule?"

"I mean the don't-sleep-around-and-don't-die-of-diseases rule."

The smile disappeared from Gretchen's face. "Is he—Does he have something?"

"I don't know."

"We should get you to the clinic." She reached for her purse.

"Gretchen, I'm not going to a clinic. If I was exposed to something, they can't undo that."

"You should still be tested. Maybe get on a preventive course of antibiotics or antivirals. And get the day-after pill."

"I'm already on the regular pill."

"You should still get tested."

"It's too soon. Nothing will show up now. Once I settle in somewhere, I'll get tested. And once every three months after that until I'm sure I'm okay."

"We could go find that cretin and make him get tested."

"No. I told you, I don't want to see him."

"Because it was so bad, or because it was so good?"

"Because I can't."

"Rina, I don't want you to leave. I'll miss you."

"I'll miss you, too."

"You're almost done with school. At least wait until graduation."

"I don't see the point."

"You might change your mind. Besides, I'll more than miss you. I need you."

"No, you don't. If anything, I need you."

"That's debatable. You'll have to stay so we can argue it out."

"I can't."

"Please don't go."

"It's not like I want to!" God, she didn't want to go. Her life was there. Pittsburgh was her home. But kind of life was it? And how could she feel safe when Ramer had already ruined the sanctuary of her home. No. It was better if she left. She chose her words carefully. "I don't know how to stay. I have some crazy guy out to get me. A gorgeous guy who used me. A cop who's implying I'm going to go down for getting attacked. A job I hate at a sketchy club. An impending—expensive—and useless degree. I've got no future here. How do I try to juggle all that? Everywhere I turn, I have another problem."

"Do you hear yourself? You just named a reason you have to stay, and you don't even remember."

"What? What reason?"

"Detective Urbani."

"Didn't you hear me? He's one of the reasons I want to go."

"He's one reason you have to stay. You promised not to leave town until his investigation was done, remember? If you leave, he might put out a warrant for your arrest."

"My arrest! I haven't done anything wrong!"

"Like you said, you're a potential suspect in his case. He just doesn't have proof yet."

"Because there's none to be found."

"Doesn't matter. If you run, you look guilty. Maybe his suspicions will turn to me as an accessory."

Rina put her head down on the table. How had this all gone to hell so quickly? Wrong place, wrong time, wrong guy. Now she was a person of interest in a crime that didn't exist, and she was the spurned one-night stand of the man of her dreams.

Somewhere along the way she must have walked under a ladder or broken a mirror.

"Ri? Rina!"

Rina lifted her head and looked at her best friend.

"I have to get to work. I'm covering for Amy. But promise me you won't leave. Not until we can figure all this out, anyway."

"I don't know. I don't want to stay in my apartment again. I still haven't fixed the window, and I'm pretty sure that's how Ramer got into my house."

Gretchen dug through her purse and produced a key.

"Stay at my place. Compared to your apartment, it's a fortress. All my windows lock tight, my door has a deadbolt, and there are usually people loitering on the street corner. They'll see if anyone enters the building who shouldn't, and they'll hear you scream—not that it'll come to that. Besides, Ramer doesn't know where I live."

"He shouldn't have known where I live, either. Clearly he has a way of finding things out."

"Just go to my place."

Rina bit her lip but didn't reach for the key.

Gretchen put the key down on the table then slid it across the surface until it sat in front of her friend. "Go. I'll see you around three. If you're awake. But I'll be quiet, just in case."

When Gretchen slid out of the booth, Rina stood, too, and wrapped her arms around her friend. "Thank you. You're the best. I don't know what I'd do without you."

Gretchen hugged her back, then stepped away. "Well, you'll never have to find out. You're staying in town, and we're going to grow old here and buy a house with a large front porch. We'll put a couple of rocking chairs out there, tend to our cats, and scare the neighborhood kids."

"I'm a dog person."

"We'll work out the details later. Right now, I have to run. Go to my place. Don't leave. Don't even look outside. And by all means, whatever you do, do not call Damien."

Gretchen left, and Rina watched her hurry down the sidewalk.

Call him? Despite her best efforts, he'd never even given her his number. She couldn't reach him if she wanted to.

The question was, did she want to?

⁂

Rina paid the bill and gathered her things. The sun sat deep on the horizon, stretching its last feeble rays into the encroaching night. She had wanted to get to Gretchen's before it was dark, but if she hurried, the best she would manage was twilight.

Still dark enough for trouble to hide in the shadows.

She rushed outside and ran right into a man walking up the street. When she plowed into him, everything he'd been carrying clattered to the ground.

"Oh, my gosh. I'm so sorry!" She bent to gather his things and bumped her head on his. She fell to one knee and rubbed her head. "I'm really sorry. Are you okay?"

He extended his hand to help her to her feet. "Better than you, I'm guessing. Are you all right? It looks like your temple is swelling."

Her gaze started at his feet and skimmed over powerful legs, trim abs, and broad shoulders until she looked up into midnight blue eyes, deep and clear as fairy tale lakes and possibly even more mesmerizing. Struck dumb, she simply stared at him.

"Miss?"

God, she was pathetic. Didn't she learn her lesson from the last hard body she obsessed over? "I'm sorry. I'm fine."

"I don't think so. How about we go inside and get you some ice?"

A refusal was on the tip of her tongue, but then she shrugged. Why the hell not? It was already dark out, so there was no reason to rush. Wasn't like she had anyone else to meet up with. What could it hurt?

"Okay. Thanks."

He smiled at her, laugh lines in the corners of his eyes crinkling to show his pleasure.

So sexy. He must smile a lot.

He opened the door and gestured for her to enter before him. When she brushed past him, she got a whiff of something exotic and decadent. Like the way she imagined the gifts of the magi to smell. Smoke and spice, wood and citrus. She paused in the doorway, closed her eyes, and breathed him in, floating on the fugue of his evocative fragrance.

"Are you light-headed? Dizzy?"

Was she ever. She opened her eyes and raised her hand to her head. Good thing she had a reason—other than her insanity—to be acting so strange. "I think I just need to sit."

He followed her through the diner, and she felt his eyes on her the whole way. When she got to the booth she had just vacated, she slid into the seat. He sat across from her.

The waitress came over. "I'm sorry. We thought you left. They've already bussed your table. I can replace your food and drink, if you'd like."

Rina shook her head. "No, that's all right. I did leave."

"Could we get some ice, please?" her companion asked. "She had an accident."

The waitress studied her face. "Oh, wow. That looks like it hurts. You want me to call an ambulance or something?"

"No, thanks." Rina's face flamed. She must look like such an idiot. Sure felt like one. "Just the ice, please."

The waitress scurried off, and the man sitting across from her reached out, cupped her chin, and lifted her face into the light. Then he frowned. "I won't ask if you're all right again, as the attention seems to bother you. But I'd be pleased if you'd do me the honor of telling me your name. I feel foolish thinking of you as the girl I injured."

"You feel foolish?" Rina looked up and met his gaze. "I'm the one who plowed into you, knocked all your things to the ground, then head-butted you when I tried to help gather everything."

The waitress returned with a bag of ice in a clean white towel and two cups of coffee. "On the house. You need anything else, just holler."

"Thanks." Rina put the ice to her head and winced, glad the waitress had already turned to leave. Her reaction didn't escape the man's notice, though.

"Hurts more than you let on, huh?"

Rina shrugged. "Let's change the topic." She extended her hand. "I'm Katarina Whitman. My friends call me Rina."

He took her hand, shook it. Held it a few seconds longer than etiquette dictated. "Pino DeAngelo. Happy to meet you."

"DeAngelo?"

"Yes." He leaned back in the book, raised an eyebrow. "Does that mean something to you?"

"Just—well, it's not that common a name. And I just met a DeAngelo."

"Oh?"

"Yes. Al. I don't suppose you know him."

"Big guy. Blond. Movie star smile?"

She dropped the ice bag. "Yeah. Yeah, that's him."

Pino laughed. "He's my brother."

"What a small world." She studied him. Was it too much of a coincidence? What were the odds? She put the ice bag back on her head.

"What is it?"

"You just don't look much alike. Same build, I suppose." Same massive, muscular, desirable build. Her cheeks flamed again, and she rushed on. "But you're so dark, and he's so fair."

His smile dimmed a bit. "He favors our father. I take after the other side."

"Well, it seems you couldn't go wrong with genes from either side of the family." What on earth was she doing? Not only flirting with yet another stranger, but complimenting his brother, too? She felt dirtier than she ever did at work, and that was saying something, given the things she'd witnessed there.

He shot her the same dazzling smile his brother had used on her when they met. Man, that was some heavenly DNA.

"So, Rina, tell me. Where were you running off to when we bumped into each other?"

Where, indeed? She could hardly remember where she was going, or why she'd been in such a hurry. Must have bumped her head harder than she thought.

"Rina?" His gaze bore into her.

She could see the concern etched on the contours of his face, and she hated to be the cause of him worrying. So she concentrated really hard, and it came to her. "I'm sorry. I was just thinking about something. Anyway, I was on my way to a friend's apartment."

"A male friend?"

She smirked. What a joke. "No. My best friend, Gretchen."

"I suppose you're in a hurry. If you're late, that is, and she's waiting for you."

"No. She's actually at work right now." Something deep inside the recesses of her muddled brain screamed a warning. She'd revealed too much information to this man. This stranger. But she just couldn't help herself. He enthralled her, and she couldn't keep her thoughts to herself. She could barely keep her emotions in check.

It rankled, but before Damien, she'd been in a bit of a man-drought. Okay, the dry spell had lingered for a few years. Now two gorgeous men were suddenly paying attention to her? It didn't seem possible. Or even probable.

Pain lanced through her head, her worries evaporated into a foggy cloud. Whatever her train of thought had been, it was suddenly gone, and she couldn't muster any concern about that.

Rina turned her attention to happier thoughts.

Pino captivated her, and he seemed just as interested in her as she was in him.

Who cared that Damien had used her as a one-night stand? She could move on just as fast as he could.

And look at what—who—she was moving on to.

"So, you have some time before anyone expects you?"

She glanced at her watch. "I do. Hours, in fact."

"Want to get out of here?"

Did she ever. "Where to?"

He stood, took her hand, and pulled her to her feet. "I know just the place."

"Lead the way."

Deep inside, a small voice screamed a warning. This wasn't like her. Not at all.

The voice was soft, so quiet it was easy to dismiss. Even though a part of her thought she should heed it, a dominant part of her brain felt otherwise. The dominant part won, and the small voice was snuffed out.

Rina followed Pino without a second thought.

She didn't know where she was going, but she couldn't wait until she got there.

Thirteen

⁌⁌

When Damien reanimated at nightfall, he flew immediately to Bar Belles. Taking human form, he went inside and looked around. Even went into the roped off sections, the restrooms, and the employees only areas.

He couldn't find Rina anywhere.

Gretchen, on the other hand, trailed him like a bloodhound.

He managed to avoid her as he scoured the club, but before he could slip outside, she cornered him near the back exit.

"You have some nerve coming in here."

"I was under the impression this was a public establishment."

"That's not what I mean, and you damn well know it."

He didn't damn well know anything, but he grew weary of the conversation. And her tone.

"Excuse me." He tried to step around her, but she blocked his way.

"Oh, no you don't."

He didn't have time for this. He was in a hurry to find

Rina, to make certain she was safe. "I'm sorry. Which is it? I shouldn't be here, or I shouldn't leave?"

"I know you're here for Rina. You've done enough damage. She doesn't want to see you. Doesn't want anything to do with you. I don't want to see you in here again. Or anywhere near her. You leave her alone, or I'll get Tiny to make you. Got it?"

He had planned to stay clear of Rina, but he thought he'd have to break her heart to do it. He had no idea what he could have done to make her want him out of her life. The night before had been the best of his life. And, being centuries old, that was saying something.

Clearly he didn't understand anything about the modern world and what people expected.

Which was just another reason for him to keep his distance.

"Not that it's any of your business, but I couldn't agree more."

"Then why in the hell are you here?"

"Like I said, it's not any of your business."

"Then I guess nothing's keeping you here." She gestured toward the door.

Tiny walked up behind her. "Everything okay here?"

"Nothing an extermination wouldn't cure," she said.

"He bothering you?"

"He bothers everybody."

Tiny turned to him, crossed his arms, flexed his muscles. "I think it's time you left."

He looked them both over then turned away without a reply.

"Probably best you don't come back," Tiny called after him.

Damien walked out the door.

He stood in the shadows of the alley and looked around. Not seeing anyone, he walked over to the dumpster and prepared for the painful transformation out of his human form. He took a deep breath and closed his eyes. Clothing tore away. Skin and bone stretched until ridges popped out on his spinal column. Claws formed on his hands and feet. Horns sprouted, as did a tail.

He shook off the agony, panted while he waited for the lingering aches to dull.

"We have a problem."

Anael's voice startled him, and not being stone, this time he did jump.

"Will you stop popping in like that?" His voice carried through the alley. "Give me warning or something."

"What's the point? My warning would surprise you as much as me appearing. It's a waste of time. Just like this conversation."

Damien closed his eyes and took a deep breath. "What do you want, Anael? I already have a bunch of problems and don't need any more. Besides, I thought you were taking a hiatus from getting involved."

"That's the thing. One of the problems I already mentioned? It's here."

"What the hell are you talking about?"

"I don't know how much I can say."

He sighed. "Well, you appeared here, so you must want to say something."

"I want to say a lot of things. I just don't know how much I can reveal before I've broken yet another rule."

"Anael, I swear to God, if—"

"Fine. Remember I told you that someone was coming to balance the scales? Well, he's here."

"We expected that."

"Yes. But I didn't expect him to break the rules."

"Why not? You did."

"I thought it would be another angel. An honorable, obedient entity."

Dread washed over Damien like an arctic waterfall. "What do you mean? Who's here?"

"My brother."

"Aren't your brothers angels?"

"He's fallen."

"A fallen angel? They—and you still haven't even told me who 'they' is—sent a fallen angel? Why?"

"I guess to actually balance things. And he's taking the balance-thing to heart. He's bent the rules, too."

"Is Rina in danger?"

"Come. We must get to her. Immediately." Anael grasped Damien's shoulder.

Before Damien could prepare, Anael transported him.

⁜

Damien's molecules reassembled in a dark alley similar to the one he'd just been in. After stifling a scream, he grabbed Anael and shoved him against a wall. "Didn't I tell you to stop doing that to me?"

"We didn't have time to fly here. Hurry. Take your human form, or we'll miss them."

"Miss who?"

"Now!"

Still not over the agony of transportation, Damien gritted his teeth against the pain of morphing from monster to man. When he was done, he looked at Anael, who once again had taken the form of Al DeAngelo.

The angel looked Damien up and down. "Couldn't you have conjured something nicer to wear?"

Damien glanced down at his clothes. He had on worn boots, ripped jeans, and an untucked button-down flannel shirt. The same type of ensemble he'd seen countless men wear on the streets of the city. Then he looked at the angel, who wore shiny loafers, tailored slacks, and a sports jacket over a silk shirt. "Do I need to change?" Did he even know how?

"Too late. We have to hurry." Anael, or Al, tugged him toward the front of the building. They rounded the corner and came face to face with Rina.

She wasn't alone.

"Rina!" Anael said. "How lovely to see you again."

"Al? What are you doing here?"

It didn't escape Damien's notice that she totally ignored him.

"Damien and I were just out for a drink. Catching up." He looked at the man with her. "Small world, seeing you here."

"Small, indeed." The man extended his hand toward Damien. "Pino DeAngelo. Al's brother. Nice to meet you."

Damien took his hand. "Damien Stone."

Pino sneered and squeezed so hard, the bones in Damien's hand rubbed together. He refused to react, but it hurt like hell.

"So," Rina said, "did the two of you just bump into each other, or did you plan on going out tonight?"

Wonder what she was getting at?

"I called him this morning, asked him to meet me," Al said. "I'm surprised he was free. If I were dating you, I'd be occupied every night."

"Oh, we're not dating," Rina said.

Damien wanted to correct her, but she was right. They weren't dating. In fact, he'd planned on keeping his distance. But hearing her state her availability so brazenly was like a knife to his back. Or his heart.

Was that why she and Gretchen were angry with him? Because he didn't offer her a commitment? Because they thought he wasn't interested in her now that he'd bedded her? They had the wrong idea. He wanted her. He just didn't deserve her.

Damien felt awful. What she must think of him.

She wasn't wrong. He was every horrible thing she could think about him. And more.

But that didn't mean he wanted her with Anael's enemy.

He tried to meet her gaze, but hers was firmly trained on Al.

"You said the two of you had lost touch. When did Damien give you his phone number? Because I tried to get it from him, and it was like trying to learn a state secret."

Ah, so that was it. He'd not only slept with her and then left without a farewell, he'd not left a way for her to contact him. It grated on him to have caused her such pain. But what could he do? He didn't have a phone.

He didn't want to give her a way to reach him, anyway. The plan was to distance himself, not make himself available to her.

"Rina," he said before Al had to lie for him, "how do you know Al's brother?"

She looked at him, her gaze frosty. Her tone even more so. "I just bumped into him outside the diner." She touched her temple. "Literally."

He looked more closely at her and saw a faint bruise on her head. "Are you all right? Do you need help getting home?"

She slipped her arm through Pino's and offered a wicked smile. "No. Thank you. I'm going with Pino. Goodnight."

They started walking, and Damien turned to Anael, pleaded silently with him to intervene.

The angel sighed, but then he reached out and grabbed his brother's arm.

Pino stopped, looked down at Anael's hand, then up into his face. When he spoke, his tone was low. "Brother?"

"I'm glad I ran into you. We have some family business to discuss."

"You could have called. I'm busy at the moment."

"I *was* about to call you."

"I thought you and Damien were out for drinks."

"We've caught up. Now you and I have some business to attend to. It's urgent."

Pino scowled at him.

Rina seemed oblivious to all of it. "I don't want to keep you from family, Pino. There's nothing more important. If I had family, I'd make them a priority. Go ahead and have your meeting. I'll be fine."

"You're not walking home alone. Especially injured."

"I'll be fine."

"At least let me call you a cab."

"Don't be ridiculous."

Damien cleared his throat. "I'll see you get home safely."

Both she and Pino opened their mouths to speak, but Anael beat them both to it. "Perfect. Damien, we'll talk later. Rina, nice seeing you again." He turned toward his brother. "Come, Pino. There's much we need to discuss, and it's getting late."

Pino took Rina's hand and kissed it. "May I call you tomorrow?"

She blushed. "I'd love that. I don't have a card—"

"Just tell me your number. I'll remember it."

She giggled, glanced at Damien, and then recited her number to Pino. "Until tomorrow, then."

"Tomorrow." He looked at Damien, and his tone grew brusque. "Damien." Then he turned and left with Al.

Damien didn't know what to make of any of that. Every fiber in him wanted to pound Pino into the ground and scream at him to stay away from Rina. But one did not fight an angel, fallen or otherwise. At least, one didn't do so and expect to win.

How was he going to protect Rina from a fallen angel? Anael wouldn't always be able to help him.

Rina started walking in the opposite direction of the

otherworldly entities, tearing Damien's attention away from his thoughts.

"Rina, wait." He darted after her.

"Don't worry about me, Damien. I can take care of myself."

"I do worry about you."

She sniffed but didn't reply.

"Where are you rushing off to? You live that way." He pointed down another street.

Rina stopped and looked up at him. "What do you want from me, Damien?"

He didn't have a clue how to answer that one, so he stared into her eyes but said nothing.

"That's what I thought." She sighed and began walking again.

"Wait." He grabbed her arm and spun her around.

Rina looked down at his hand, then up into his face. "Let go of me."

He dropped her arm. "I'm worried about you."

"You haven't earned the right to worry about me."

"After last night, I think I have a vested interest in your wellbeing."

"Sleeping with someone doesn't give you a 'vested interest' in them. Being involved with them does. And you made it perfectly clear we're not involved."

"How the hell did I do that?"

"You left!" When the few pedestrians out at that hour looked their way, she lowered her voice and pulled him against a building, out of the glow of the streetlight above them. "You snuck out in the middle of the night. Didn't leave a number. Didn't say you'd call. Your note was basically a Dear John letter. You have no right following me. Or stopping me from seeing someone else."

"I didn't sneak out. I left. I didn't want to wake you, so I left a note."

"You didn't leave your number."

Kind of hard to argue that. "Well, you didn't give me yours, either."

She growled her frustration. "Damien, what do you want from me?"

How to answer that? He had been so sure he wanted to keep his distance, but he'd just spent the last five minutes trying to convince her to stay with him. The whole reason he'd decided to cut ties with her was because she deserved better than him.

"What do you want from me?" he countered.

She frowned. "No. I'm not playing these games with you. I slept with you. That's something you might not take seriously, but it's a big deal for me. You know where I stand. You know how I feel, you know where I live. You know a lot about me, more than most people do. Now the burden is on you. What. Do. You. Want?"

"I want you to be safe."

"Well, then, you're in luck. Because between Gretchen, Tiny, and Pino, I think I'm in good shape."

"That's why Ramer keeps getting to you." Low blow, but he didn't know what else to do.

Rina pursed her lips, then she seemed to deflate. "You're worried about my safety?"

He nodded.

"I want you to get tested."

"Tested?"

She rolled her eyes. "Tested. For STDs."

He had no idea what that meant, but the way she said it, he gathered he was supposed to. Just another way he didn't fit into her world. He wasn't fluent in the language. He'd ask Anael later but needed to find a way to continue the conversation now.

"What for?"

"What for? So I know you're clean. We slept together.

Without protection. For all I know, you sleep with a different woman every day. Lord only knows what diseases you're carrying around with you. If I caught something off you, I want to know."

He still didn't know what the letters stood for, but he got the gist of her concern. "You didn't catch anything from me. You're safe."

"Yeah, well, forgive me if I don't take your word for it. I'd rather hear a doctor tell me."

"Rina, I don't sleep around. In fact, I'd bet my life that before we spent the night together, you'd had sex more recently than I have. Maybe I should ask you to get tested."

"That's absurd."

"I'm not the one who was going home with another member of the opposite sex tonight."

"We were walking together. That doesn't mean I was going to sleep with him."

"Doesn't mean you weren't going to, either. I saw the way you looked at him."

She opened her mouth, closed it again. Finally she said, "You know, I don't owe you an explanation for who I spend my time with."

"Now who isn't taking last night seriously?"

"Goodbye, Damien." She started to walk away.

"Wait."

She didn't.

Again he hurried to catch up to her. "I can't let you walk around in the dark with Ramer looking for you."

Rina looked mutinous, and he feared she was going to cause a scene. Instead, she shrugged. "You want to see me home safely? Fine. But don't expect an invitation upstairs."

"Why are you so mad at me?"

She turned to stare at him, mouth agape. Then she shook her head and kept walking.

It was the quietest, tensest walk of his life. She didn't utter a single word.

And he didn't have a clue what to say to make things between them better.

⁘

After seeing Rina safely to Gretchen's, and making sure no one followed them, he transformed then flew back to his roof. He didn't know where else to go.

Once he got there, he regretted his decision.

Anael and Pino stood there. Apparently waiting for him.

"I have a few hours before sunrise. I'd rather spend them alone, if you don't mind."

"You let this... abomination dictate his wishes to you?" Pino asked Anael. "No wonder I've been sent to set things right."

Rage roiled through Damien. He might not be able to take an angel—fallen or otherwise—but he wouldn't stand to be insulted by one. He bared his claws and rounded on Pino, but Anael stepped between them and pushed him back.

"Damien, please turn back into your human form. My brother might find you easier to talk to that way."

Damien didn't care what Pino found easy. It hurt like hell to morph. And he didn't see why he needed to endure the pain just to make things easier for the fallen.

"Can't stand a little twinge?" Pino taunted. "Weak."

Damien ground his teeth and assumed human form. Tried not to let his expression register the pain.

Pino laughed. "Pathetic."

Damn mind-readers. "Stay the fuck out of my head."

"Nothing interesting in there, anyway."

Again Damien went to charge at him, and again Anael intervened.

"Damien, this is my brother, Penemuel. He's been dispatched to counteract the rules I've broken."

"You want to tell me how seducing Rina settles the score?"

Penemuel shrugged, picked non-existent lint off what was undoubtedly a designer shirt. "You slept with her."

"I'm supposed to. You're not. You're not even human!"

The fallen raised a brow. "Seriously? That argument, coming from you?"

Damien huffed, gritted his teeth. Struggled for a sense of calm he could only imagine. Finally, he spoke in a soft, controlled voice. "She's my destiny, not yours."

The fallen pierced him with a dark stare. "But you weren't supposed to deceive her in your fated quest, were you?"

"What was I supposed to do? Show her that gargoyles are real?"

"Not my problem."

"Stay away from her." Damien's tone rose, sharpened.

"Or what?"

Anael stepped between them. "Okay. Everybody cool down. I think it's safe to say we've all made a mistake or two. What matters now is how we proceed from here."

"I've made no mistakes. I'm doing what I was sent here to do. And I'll proceed however I damn well see fit." At that, Penemuel vanished.

Anael hung his head and closed his eyes.

"What's his story?"

"He's angry because he's been kicked out of Heaven."

"Isn't that kind of the definition of the fallen?"

"Most of the fallen fell because they were jealous that God had elevated humans. They felt they were superior beings and wanted power for themselves."

"I know that. Everyone knows that."

Anael shook his head. "That's not what happened to Penemuel. He liked humans. Tried to help them."

"Yeah? How?"

"He taught them to write. Humans weren't supposed to be given that knowledge. He was punished for it. Banished."

"If he was banished, how did God—or whoever is pulling the strings—get him to come down here? Up here? Whatever."

"He was already here. I suppose when he was offered the opportunity to intervene, maybe stick it to an angel, he jumped at the chance."

"Are you ever going to tell me who your immediate boss is? God isn't answering my prayers, but if I could just meet with your superiors, explain I didn't understand, then—"

"That's all immaterial now. Things are too far along. We're just going to have to see this through and hope things work out for us both."

"You're pitting me against someone with supernatural powers. Formerly angelic powers."

"Not formerly. His powers have not changed."

Damien bit back a curse. "He's actively working to keep me and Rina apart."

"Funny it has you so worked up, seeing as you were planning on walking away from her."

"That was to protect her. Now that she has a fallen after her, as well as Ramer, I seem to be her only chance."

"Better late than never, I guess."

Damien looked out over the city, wondering what Rina was doing at that moment. Was Ramer looking for her? Had Penemuel found her? What did he plan on doing with her, anyway?

"Anael? What happens to Rina if Penemuel wins?"

"Let's not worry about that unless it actually happens."

Damien turned to look at him, but he'd already gone.

Fourteen

⁓

Rina stewed at Gretchen's for several hours. She tried watching television, making a snack, listening to music, reading. Drinking.

Nothing took her mind off Damien and Pino.

So it was weird that she hadn't had a date in months, and now she had two guys she was interested in. Guys who were associated with each other in some way—through Al, a third guy she'd met out of the blue.

Not all coincidences were suspect, were they?

She couldn't help but feel, on some level, she wouldn't have met any of them had it not been for Ramer. Not that she'd thank him.

But having to choose between two of the best looking guys she'd ever seen wasn't quite a hardship.

Who was she kidding? She had many more pressing problems than which guy to be with. She wasn't sure either of them really wanted her, anyway.

Damn it. She should have just left town.

By the time Gretchen got home, Rina was well past buzzed, fully into drunk-territory.

Which made her weepy. And wobbly.

"How much wine have you had?" Gretchen asked.

There was a question. How much had she had? She vaguely remembered the first bottle. Had hurt her hand opening the second. She tried to wiggle her fingers, couldn't feel a thing. She giggled.

"What's so funny?" Gretchen asked.

Rina couldn't say. But it was hilarious. She grabbed the bottle with her injured hand and tried to pour more wine into her glass. Missed. Didn't matter, though. The bottle was empty. A drop of burgundy landed on her shoe, and she fell over trying to wipe it off.

"Oh, man. You are wasted." Gretchen studied her. "Are you hurt? Looks like you bumped your head on something."

"My hand." She wiggled her fingers at her friend and laughed again.

"Your hand is swollen. Not as bad as your head, though. What'd you do?"

"I fell."

"Let's get some ice on your head." Gretchen walked into the kitchen.

Rina shook her head. The room spun, and she put down her hand to steady herself. A small throb reverberated through her palm, and she squinted at it. How the hell had she hurt her hand opening a bottle?

"Here." Gretchen held ice to her head as she squatted beside her.

Rina grabbed the bag and put it on her hand. "Already had ice on my head. Pino gave it to me."

"The wine gave you ice for your head?"

"What?"

Gretchen grabbed the empty bottle and turned the label toward her friend. "Pinot noir gave you ice?"

Rina burst into gales of laughter. She pictured the bottle hopping onto a stool and grabbing ice from the freezer. Wine bottles with hands and feet were funny. Wine bottles with hands and feet dressed like a butler were hysterical.

When she calmed down, she waved her injured hand, felt the throb of the movement. Seemed the grape elixir was wearing off. She shook her head. "No. Not the wine." A smirk escaped her, and she tried not to think about the butler-bottle. "I ran into a guy named Pino."

"Pino? Pino who?"

"Literally ran right into him." She pointed at her head.

"You aren't making any sense. I'm going to make coffee, and you're going to start at the beginning."

Picturing a coffee cup in a maid's outfit bustling after the wine-bottle butler made her laugh all over again. Gretchen sighed and walked into the kitchen.

When Rina calmed, she clambered to her feet and made her way to the dinette. Plopped down on the wooden chair. Maybe a little too hard. Kind of hurt her tailbone.

Sobered her a little bit, though.

Gretchen joined her at the table and placed a mug of black coffee in front of her. "Now. Explain. From the beginning."

She sipped the scalding liquid and began to tell the story. Probably took three times as long to get through it than if she had been logical and sober, but the good news was that by the time she was done, the wine had worn off enough that she could process information again.

"What are you saying? You think Ramer put these guys up to meeting you?"

"Hmm?" Okay, maybe she wasn't at one hundred percent yet.

"You said these three guys are all somehow involved with each other, and that you didn't meet any of them until after Ramer assaulted you. Are you saying you think he sent them?"

"Why would he do that?"

"I don't know. I thought that was your theory."

Was it?

"They could be like spies infiltrating the enemy camp."

Rina thought for a minute. Thinking hurt. Her head had begun to pound, and she felt a little queasy. But she needed to make sense of things. "No. That can't be it. Damien saved me from Ramer that first night. No way could Ramer have sent him."

"What about Al and Pino, then?"

She sipped her coffee. Her stomach lurched. "Why? Why would Ramer send people Damien knows? Besides, there's some tension there. These guys... I don't know. It's like they don't get along but act like they do, or something."

"Some kind of family drama?"

"I guess."

"What's that have to do with Damien? Or Ramer?"

"Ramer? Nothing I can think of. Damien, though? Maybe he's the reason the brothers are fighting. Like he's closer to Al than Pino is, and that made Pino jealous. Hurt his feelings. Although, I think they just met tonight, so... I don't know."

Gretchen refilled Rina's mug. "Well, if Pino's feelings are hurt, that just makes me hate Damien more. And like Pino more."

"You never even met Pino."

"Doesn't matter. Damien used you."

"That's not what he says."

"Okay, what did the slime ball say?"

Rina sipped her drink and thought back over their conversation, but the details were fuzzy. They'd stood on the sidewalk and argued over safety and sex. Over whether he was interested in her or not. But she couldn't remember them coming to any consensus. And they didn't talk at all on the way home.

"Well?" Gretchen asked.

"I don't know. My head hurts."

"Get to bed. We'll figure it out in the morning."

"After all this coffee? I'll be up all night."

"Well, I'm wiped. I'm going to bed. You staying in my room or on the couch?"

"Couch. I don't want to keep you up."

"Fine." Gretchen stood and headed toward her bedroom. "Just stay out of the liquor. You're going to be miserable in the morning."

Fat lot she knew. Rina was already miserable.

Rina woke with a dry mouth and dry heaves. At least she didn't puke, but every retch sent an ice pick through her brain.

She hadn't thought she'd fall asleep the night before, but she couldn't even remember lying down. Must have passed out.

Wished she would again.

"Good morning, sunshine!" Gretchen called when she walked into the living room.

"Shh." Rina sat gingerly on the edge of the sofa and rubbed her temples.

"Thought you might feel this way. Want me to make you my patented hangover cure?"

"Does it have morphine in it?"

She laughed. "No. It's got a raw egg, pickle juice, a—"

"God, stop." Rina's stomach flopped.

"How about a piece of toast?"

She groaned. Didn't matter what Gretchen thought that meant. That was the only noise she had the energy to make. Rina picked her way to the table, each delicate step making her head throb and stomach flip.

"So, I was thinking." Gretchen slid the toaster's lever down.

The *whoosh-click* of the mechanism echoed painfully in Rina's head, and she cringed. She sat and rubbed her temples again. When Gretchen started to speak, Rina held her finger up to stop her. After a few minutes, she looked up and managed to whisper, "What?"

"You know Damien's on my shit-list."

"I don't know if—"

"Not finished." The toast popped up. Gretchen grabbed a piece and slathered butter on it. "It was nice of him to come to your rescue, and all, but it just feels like he's a player. If he really cared, he wouldn't have skipped out."

"I never really gave him a chance to explain."

"There is no good explanation." She slid two plates of toast on the table. "Jelly?"

"God, no."

She stepped into the kitchen, returned with a jar of apple jelly, then smeared some on her toast. "When a guy cuts out and has an excuse—and trust me, there are very few good excuses for doing that—he better leave a note."

"Damien did leave a note."

"More like a goodbye than a reason for leaving. Anyway, it got me thinking."

Rina took a bite of toast, prayed it stayed down.

"It doesn't matter if his intentions were good when he helped you. Maybe he's a Good Samaritan, maybe he's former military—"

"That would explain the haircut."

"Maybe he's a bouncer by trade and it was just a knee-jerk reaction. It doesn't matter. None of that makes up for him using you."

"I still don't know if I'd say he used me."

"This Pino guy? What's his deal?"

"What do you mean? I told you, I just met him."

"But there was a connection, right?"

Rina sighed. "It wasn't a connection, exactly. It was more like—"

"Like what?"

"It's hard to explain. When I was with him, it was almost

like I was obsessed. Thinking back on it, it doesn't make sense. But at the time, I was enthralled."

"What? You mean, like when moron damsels in distress succumb to the thrall of a vampire?"

"This isn't fiction. I wasn't compelled by a supernatural creature."

"Maybe he hypnotized you."

"I don't believe in that, either."

"You need a little whimsy in your life."

"I need less excitement, not more."

"Don't you believe in love at first sight?"

"Sure. In romance novels and fairy tales."

"Damien might have been your savior, but it sounds like Pino is the one you're drawn to."

"You didn't see Damien's abs," Rina mumbled.

"What?"

"Nothing."

"I just think you need to put Damien on the back burner and see what you can heat up with Pino."

"You haven't even met him."

"I don't think I have to. There's something there. You want my advice?"

"Probably not."

"See where things go with Pino and forget about Damien. Cut him loose. Keep your distance."

"I still have to see him. He's involved in the investigation. And I asked him to get tested. I have to see him to get his results."

"He agreed to get tested?"

Rina thought about it. "Actually, no. At least, I don't think so. Maybe. I don't know. He didn't really refuse, but he told me I'd had sex more recently than him, so the burden of proving health was on me."

"Are you kidding me? Look at the guy. Are we supposed to believe he's a monk or something? Not looking like that."

"I don't know." Her head still pounded.

"Of course, given his personality, I can see where women would run screaming."

"I didn't."

"You aren't the best judge of character."

"I'm friends with you."

"I'll let that one slide, given you're hung over."

"Great."

"Listen, put Damien on hold. Give Pino a whirl. Well, maybe not a literal one. At least, not on the first date. And not without protection, this time."

"I hate you."

"You love me." Gretchen finished her toast and stood up. "Why don't you give him a call? See what this attraction-thing is really all about?"

Rina rested her head on the table. What a loser she was. Two guys now, and both times she'd failed to get a phone number.

"Hey," Gretchen said. "Your phone's ringing."

"Probably that detective. Let it go to voice mail."

"Might be Pino." Gretchen ran into the living room and rooted through Rina's purse.

"I think you're the one obsessed. I'm not ready for a relationship with anyone. I can barely sit up right now."

But Gretchen ignored her and returned with Rina's phone.

She looked at caller ID. Didn't say the police station. Didn't say anything at all.

"Answer it!"

What the hell. She swiped her finger across the screen. "Hello."

"Hello, Rina? It's Pino DeAngelo."

She smiled. "Hi, Pino."

"Put it on speaker." Gretchen waggled her eyebrows and stuck her tongue out.

Rina shook her head and held her finger to her lips to shush her.

She grinned. "See? Destiny. Make a date."

Rina swatted at her and turned her attention back to Pino. "What's up?"

"I was thinking about you. I know it's early, but I didn't want you to think I wasn't going to call."

"I wasn't worried." Liar. She had been worried he wouldn't call. And then he did call, and she worried about why.

"I promise, I have nothing but the best of intentions. I thought you might like to grab a bite to eat tonight. I'd really like to take you out, get to know you better."

It was like he read her thoughts. All she'd done was think about him, and he called. She'd been curious about his motives, and he volunteered them. By asking her out! Presumably to get to know her better.

Was it creepy, or was it a sign?

Guess she'd figure it out on their date. Despite her reservations, she couldn't say no.

Fifteen

Damien had spent the night pacing on the roof, alternating between being pissed off and confused. Spent the day petrified on his plinth, feeling the same way.

When night fell again, he stretched his wings and took flight. Soaring through the sky didn't make things any less frustrating or convoluted, but it felt good to fly. Had to make sure no one saw him, though, so he coasted above the clouds on a wing and a prayer.

Well, a wing, anyway.

He came upon the confluence at the Point and decided a bath would reinvigorate him, so he took a nose dive into the river underneath the Fort Pitt bridge. The water was dark and deep, providing him with cover from prying eyes. No one but the fish knew he was there, and they didn't seem to mind. After scrubbing away a day's accumulation of dirt, he even played with a few catfish before resurfacing and heading home.

What he was going to do all night on the roof of Nathaniel Burton Mansion was anyone's guess.

He never made it there, though.

Instead, he found himself assuming human form and walking in the front door of Bar Belles.

His vision grew accustomed to the dark, and he scanned the room. The stage had three girls on it in various stages of undress. He'd never seen so much glitter. Or so much skin exposed in a public place. Not that he was a prude, but he averted his eyes.

They weren't who he was looking for, and they did nothing for him.

Tiny stood near the stage, bulky arms crossed—his favorite pose.

Damien nodded at him but got no response.

Wonder if he didn't see him or this was still attitude from the night before.

Knowing Tiny's hyper-vigilance, Damien figured he saw him. Gretchen didn't make decisions for Rina, so the cold reception meant Rina had probably complained about him. He sighed. The modern world was far more difficult than the thirteenth century.

He turned toward the bar, hoping to see Rina there. Instead, Gretchen wove her way through the crowd, heading straight for him. Maybe she had gotten through to Tiny.

"She doesn't want to see you."

He looked down at her. She held her empty tray almost like a shield in front of her, but she stood her ground.

"I think that's for her to say, not you."

Gretchen shrugged. "Suit yourself. She switched shifts with Bailey, so she's just getting off work now. She's in the back, changing."

"Can you tell her I'm out here? Please?"

"No need. She's not leaving out the back. She's meeting her date by the door." Gretchen gave him a saccharine smile then headed toward the bar.

Date?

Damien turned around and scanned the few tables set

back by the door. One was empty. One had a dancer propositioning a couple of frat boys. He doubted Rina would be interested in any of them.

The last one back there had one man sitting at it. He sat back against the wall, his features cast in shadow. Damien headed toward him, the only person who could be the mysterious date, then the man leaned into the dim lighting of the room. It stopped Damien in mid-step.

Penemuel.

Damien growled low in his throat and stalked over to the table.

The fallen sat there, twirling a pen through his fingers. "I'd offer you a seat, but I think I'll be leaving shortly."

"Why are you doing this?"

"You know why."

"But you don't even care about her. You're just using her to screw me over."

Penemuel shrugged. "She's like whipped cream and a cherry on top of my dessert. And we all know about women and whipped cream."

Damien's brows drew down. He had no idea what that meant.

The fallen shrugged. "Or maybe we don't all know. I keep forgetting you aren't familiar with this world."

"I'm familiar with it. I've been observing it for centuries."

Penemuel stood and patted Damien's cheek. He flinched away.

"You may have kept watch over the world, Damien, but you haven't lived in it. You may know what a car is, but you've never driven one. You have heard the changes in language, but you don't always speak in the modern vernacular. Hell, you don't even have a computer or a phone."

Damn him, but he was right. Damien hadn't given Rina his number or promised to call her, not because he didn't want to, but because he didn't have the means. Maybe not even the knowledge.

"You can wish to damn me all you want, Damien. It's a waste of your time. I was damned eons before your birth. I've got nothing more to lose, and nothing but time at my disposal."

Rage surged through Damien like a tide gushing through a fiord. "Stay the fuck out of my head, Penemuel."

"Or what?"

"Or I'll find a way to kick your ass." That sounded like modern language, asshole. "And stay the fuck away from Katarina."

"Just who do you think you are to dictate who can be involved with me and who can't?"

Rina's voice, tinged with anger and incredulity, carried over the club's music from behind him. He could tell by the smirk on Penemuel's face that he'd been baited into saying that right when Rina would hear it. He turned around.

"Rina, I—"

"Save it. I hope you aren't here for me. I have plans. Now, if you'll excuse us." She reached for Penemuel's hand,. He took hers then placed a kiss on it.

Bastard.

They headed for the door without even glancing back at him. He heard Penemuel's laughter ringing inside his head.

Biting back an oath, he rushed after them. He stepped out of the club and blinked, trying to acclimate to the brightness of the streetlight above him. Just as he was about to turn and follow them up the street, he caught movement out of the corner of his eye. He turned in time to see Dylan Ramer and one of his lackeys rushing at Rina and Penemuel, who had their backs to their attackers and appeared to be unaware of the imminent danger.

He thought a warning to the fallen a split second before he yelled it aloud.

But his timing was off. He rushed at the attackers, but Ramer reached Rina first and knocked her to the ground. She lay there, unconscious, and Ramer fell beside her.

While Damien battled Ramer's henchman, he trusted the fallen to protect Rina. So he turned his attention to his own battle, fought as though possessed. An elbow, an uppercut, a jab and a cross, then the guy was out cold.

Ramer was climbing back to his feet, and Penemuel just stood there, uninvolved and unaffected. Damien lunged at Ramer, but he stepped aside. Damien recovered and looked at Ramer, who gave a quick glance to both him and Penemuel, then he ran, not even bothering to stop and help his cohort.

Damien heard a soft thunk, like the sound of the door behind him closing, but when he turned, no one had come onto the street. Satisfied Rina wasn't in danger, he turned his attention back to her. He bent to one knee to tend to her. Patted her cheek, rubbed her hand. When she began to stir, Penemuel knelt beside her and snatched her hand from his.

"Are you all right?" Penemuel asked.

Damien stared into her eyes even though the fallen had her hand and her attention. She looked lucid enough, her eyes seemed clear even though her expression was one of confusion.

"What happened?" she asked.

"We were attacked," Penemuel said. "You were hit from behind and knocked down. I subdued this attacker, but I'm afraid the other man got away."

What? *He* fought the attackers off?

"You fought two of them off? By yourself?"

"It was nothing. My only concern was your safety."

Damien swore a blue streak in his head, only to hear Penemuel's laughter and taunting in reply.

"Oh, Pino," she said. "How can I ever thank you?"

"Rina," Damien said. "It was Ramer. You need to call the police."

"You call the police. I want to thank Pino for saving me." She pulled Pino's head down and kissed him.

Damien had never seen that shade of red before. His blood pumped so hot in his veins, it made the fires of hell feel cold.

Anael appeared beside him, grabbed his arm, then pulled him back before he did something foolish.

Again he heard laughter in his head.

"Katarina," Anael said. "Do you need medical attention? You have a nasty bruise on your head."

She stepped away from Penemuel. "Al? What are you doing here?"

"I was meeting Damien. I happened to be walking up the street and saw what happened. I only wish I had been here in time to lend a hand."

She brushed her clothes off and straightened them. "Your brother was a hero."

"My brother?" He raised an eyebrow.

"Didn't you see him fight both men off?" She glared at Damien. "By himself?"

"I thought it was Damien."

She sniffed. "Well, you were far away. I suppose in the dark that mistake was easy enough to make."

Damien turned to Anael, pleaded with his eyes. Asked for help in his thoughts.

Anael shrugged.

"Well, I don't want to delay you boys. You should get going. Unless you want to answer more questions from the police?"

"I, uh—" Damien had no idea how to proceed. "I didn't call them."

She sighed. "Why would you? You don't seem to call anyone when you're supposed to."

Penemuel held up a phone. "Don't worry, darling. I called them."

Darling? Please, no. Surely Katarina wouldn't fall for such blatantly false endearments.

"Thank you, Pino." She slipped her arm through his. "Damien, I think you'd better go."

"Perhaps he should stay," Anael said. "The police may wish to talk with him."

"Why? He didn't do anything. I'm sure Pino's statement will suffice."

"Multiple witnesses are better than just one," Anael said.

She sighed. "Please, just go. I can't deal with this right now."

Damien's heart broke a little. His soul perhaps a little more. But he couldn't hurt her further. He turned and walked away, fighting against taking even one glance back at her.

Again, Penemuel's laughter rang in his head.

⚜

Damien heard Anael's footsteps hurrying after him, heard him inside his head telling him to wait.

He didn't.

He kept stomping down the street, looking for a corner dark enough to transform in and fly away.

Or for something to pummel. That would work, too.

A police car with flashing lights went up the street. Didn't zoom, didn't speed. Looked more like a guy out for a Sunday drive, except the lights were on. Not even a siren. Damien turned and saw the car stop in front of Bar Belles. It was a damn good thing Rina wasn't in need of emergency help. Bastard certainly wasn't in a hurry to get to her.

Anael caught up to him.

"Is my time up?"

"What?" The angel looked at him, his usually beatific face drawn in a worried frown. "Time for what?"

"I lost, right? Penemuel won her affections. I go to hell. Isn't that the deal?"

"It's a bit more complicated than that, Damien. Besides, he hasn't *won* anything yet."

"She's out with him, not me. That seems like a loss."

"In more ways than one, I'm sure."

Damien scowled at him.

"Haven't you speculated about that?"

"What?"

"About how she just abandoned any feelings she had for you and immediately fell for him?"

"I would assume it's because I can't call her. Or drive her anywhere. Or discuss anything with an air of knowledge. Or stay with her past dawn. Penemuel can do all of it. What he can't do, he can magically manipulate."

"I'd focus on the manipulation part, if I were you."

"Why?" Damien kicked a pebble and watched it skip over the sidewalk then fall into the gutter. He knew just what that little stone felt like.

"Damien, I'm already in trouble for interfering as much as I have. That's why Penemuel is here. I can't say anything more. Just—just think about what I said. Focus on the manipulation. And go see Katarina. You haven't lost yet. Don't make things any easier on him." With that, Anael vanished.

Damien didn't know what that daft old angel meant about Penemuel and manipulation. Nor did he care. He was looking at an eternity in hell, all because he hadn't made up his mind fast enough. And now his time was limited, Rina was in danger, and...

And Penemuel would probably be the one to drag him into the fire.

Well, if he was damned, he might as well throw caution to the wind and enjoy himself before he went.

He turned and headed up the street.

Sixteen

❧

Rina rolled her eyes when the police showed up. There was an officer who looked like he didn't want to be there—and probably didn't. Who could blame him? Detective Urbani arrived in a black SUV, got out of the car, then immediately laid into the first responder about something.

She shook her head. Glad the guy was in a good mood.

"Miss Whitman. More troubles, I see."

"Don't you ever take a shift off?"

"I told you the last time we had occasion to meet. This case has been given top priority by people higher up the ladder than I am. Looks like we'll be seeing a lot of each other until this matter is resolved."

"I changed my mind. I don't want to make a statement." She started walking.

"Miss Whitman." The detective grabbed her arm and spun her around.

Her eyes widened. She looked at the detective's hand on her arm, then up into his eyes. Fear flooded through her. It wasn't until that moment that she realized she could end up in that police car. In a cell. In court and in prison.

Terrified, her teeth chattered, and she wove on her feet.

"I'd thank you to unhand the lady."

She looked from the detective to the man beside her. Pino. She'd forgotten he was there. But there he was, a formidable presence. Even the detective dropped her arm and backed off a little.

"I'm not the problem here, pal," Urbani said.

"Apparently you are to her. Do you make a habit of intimidating victims?"

"You don't know the extenuating circumstances here."

"I don't need to." Pino stood taller, seemed to grow broader at the same time. "I called in the assault. This lady was the victim. So take our statements, or we can go downtown and talk to your boss."

"You really don't want to do that," the detective said.

"And you really don't want to force my hand."

Urbani went a bit slack-jawed, blinked a few times. When he spoke, his voice sounded monotonous and inattentive. "I'm not needed here. Officer?"

The bored officer looked up, pushed off the car he was leaning on, then walked over. "Yeah?"

Urbani glared at him. "Take their statements. Give them a ride home, make sure they get there safely."

"Sir." The officer nodded, his tone far more demure than that of his earlier insubordinate comment.

The detective shook his head, furrowed his brow, and left without a backward glance.

Rina was confused at the shift in his attitude, but she couldn't dwell on it. She had to give her account to the officer, who stood there with a pad and pen, waiting.

She thought back over the events of the night, thought about what Pino told her had happened. What Al thought he'd seen.

About Damien and his reaction.

Something wasn't right with this whole thing. Her

thoughts were fuzzy, and the more she tried to clarify them, the harder it was to bring them into focus.

"Rina? The officer asked you a question." Pino stood there, staring at her.

She couldn't read the expression on his face. Instead, she turned toward the officer and began telling her blurry version of the attack.

When she got to the part about Pino single-handedly saving her, she swore he sneered.

Something was definitely wrong. And she was determined to find out what.

Rina didn't talk much on the way to her apartment. She mulled over everything that had happened—from the first assault through all the subsequent attacks, to the threats and comments Urbani had made, to the coincidence of all the men coming into her life at once.

Then there was the strange dream she'd had. Also, the weird inklings she felt when Pino got involved in things.

She squeezed the bridge of her nose. Her head pounded and her thoughts grew muddled every time she tried to think about it.

"Are you okay?" Pino asked.

"Fine. Just a bit of a headache. Long night." She didn't look at him. Maybe he thought she was making excuses so she didn't have to ask him up. Not that she needed an excuse. No one was entitled to an invitation into her home. Or bed. He could think what he wanted. She didn't care.

She needed a break. Time away from all these men, all these problems.

Should have run when she wanted to. Why did she listen to Gretchen and stay?

Oh, right. Because Urbani told her not to leave. She was under investigation.

Which cycled her back to the beginning, and she went through all of it again.

Something unified all of it. She just couldn't quite put the picture together without that one missing puzzle piece.

When they arrived at her apartment, she turned to look at Pino. No doubt about it, he was gorgeous. That he wanted to spend time with her was flattering. It also didn't quite track.

"This is me." She gestured at her apartment. "So much for our date."

He shrugged. "It certainly wasn't what I'd imagined when I asked you out. But you're safe, and we had a lovely walk back here."

"Yes, we did." Okay, she didn't handle silences well on a good day. Awkward silences after such a stressful night? She wanted to jump out of her skin.

"Okay, well, ah… I guess this is it. Goodnight." She turned and hurried toward the door.

"Rina."

She didn't want to, knew her willpower might buckle under the weight of his penetrating stare, but she turned anyway. Looked him straight in the eyes. His mesmerizing, hypnotic, indigo eyes.

Somehow, her feet carried her back to him. She didn't want to. She wanted to run and hide inside. But there she stood, inches from him, looking up at—

His lips. They looked so soft, so firm. So utterly kissable and likely delectable.

What the hell was wrong with her?

"I gotta go." She whirled around, but he grasped her arm, spun her back to face him.

"What's wrong? Where are you rushing off to?"

"I need to get inside."

"You're safe with me. Ramer isn't here. Even if he was, I

wouldn't let him get to you. You know that, right? You remember how I defended you?"

She didn't. The night was a blur, the details changing and morphing into different people, different actions.

"I won't feel safe with anyone until this is over. I'm sorry, Pino. I'm just not in a place right now where I can be involved with anyone. Not until I've moved past all this."

"Rina, it's okay."

"I'm sorry. Also grateful. But right now, I just need some sleep. Goodnight, Pino."

She crossed the street, reached for the door handle.

"Rina!" Pino called.

With a sigh, she turned.

"If you're worried about your safety, I'd suggest you get that window fixed." He waved then headed up the street.

It wasn't until she entered her apartment that it hit her.

He shouldn't know which window was hers.

⁘

Rina sat in her apartment, completely confused about her next step. She should have gone to Gretchen's. Her broken window made her nervous enough. Pino mentioning it only magnified her discomfort.

Instead of leaving, she poured herself a generous glass of wine. When she curled up on the sofa, she flipped on the television. The burned-out pixels mocked her, each dot a reminder of the trouble she'd caused herself by her late-night drunken shopping spree. Rina stabbed the off button—with a little more force than necessary—then drained her glass.

She didn't know what to do. About anything. Pondering her legal troubles did nothing for her. That whole matter was out of her control.

Her man troubles weren't much easier to manage.

On paper, Pino looked like the perfect man. In reality,

something didn't add up. How much did she actually know about him, anyway? His name, his brother... that he had smoldering good looks? Those things certainly weren't enough to make a decision on.

Of course, she knew little more than that about Damien, and she'd slept with him. But despite the mystery, she sensed something in him. Honor. Valor. Dependability.

It didn't hurt that he was also drop dead gorgeous.

She poured more wine.

Should she give Damien another chance? He didn't seem as mysterious as Pino. Rather, his mysteries seemed a little less... ominous.

Ultimately, she decided that wouldn't be a good idea. She couldn't give herself to a man—to a relationship—that was so one-sided. She talked, he listened. She got in trouble, he stepped in to help. What she needed reciprocity. She wanted him to open up about his life, his history, his dreams and desires. Also, she needed equality. She wanted to be there for him when he needed her, whatever problem he faced. Otherwise, she was nothing more than a damsel in distress. Not to mention a convenient roll in the hay.

Two things she swore she'd never be.

Maybe it was too late. Maybe she'd already become both.

Ugh, men infuriated her.

The doorbell rang, startling her. She sloshed a bit of wine on her leg when she jumped and swore under her breath. What a waste of wine. What a pain the laundry would be.

"Maybe it's my new television, and I can watch something without the reminder of what a moron I am."

She walked to the door, grabbed the handle, and got ready to unlock the dead bolt. Then she paused. Just because she wanted it to be the TV didn't mean it was. Especially at that hour of the night.

More likely it would be Ramer.

Who was she kidding? He used her damn window last

time and would likely do so again. The thought made her shiver.

Of course, danger didn't knock. Did it?

No way to know but to check.

She stood on her toes, looked through the peephole, then she flung open the door.

"Damien? What are you doing here?"

"I thought we could talk. Are you alone?" He looked over her head into the room beyond.

"Pino isn't here, if that's what you're wondering."

He shrugged. "Doesn't matter what I was thinking."

"Seems to be a theme with you," she muttered.

"What?"

"Never mind. You checked on me. You see I'm alone. You know I'm relatively safe. You can go."

She started to close the door, put he put his hand out and stopped her.

"I'm glad you're safe. But I meant it. I want to talk."

Will wonders ever cease? She opened the door wider and gestured him inside.

Seventeen

⚬᥎⚬

Damien looked at the wine bottle and glass. Singular. One glass. So she hadn't lied. Not only wasn't Penemuel there, he hadn't been there.

Not that he thought she'd lie. She wouldn't. It was just nice to know she hadn't invited him up.

Of course, that meant the fallen had left her alone. Unprotected. And on the same night Ramer had attacked her again, too.

Bastard.

"Have a seat." Rina gestured to the sofa. When he sat, she continued into the kitchen. A moment later, she returned with a glass and wine bottle. She topped off her glass, filled his, then handed it to him.

His fingers brushed hers when he took it. Chills skittered up his arm. He didn't know why he'd ever thought of leaving her. She was his. He felt it deep in his soul. He didn't want to be with her to avoid damnation—although that was a hell of a bonus. He wanted to be with her because she was his breath, his pulse, his life. Avoiding her to protect her was cowardly. Once he honestly approached the possibility of a life with her, he knew one unavoidable truth.

It was a necessity.

And he couldn't make it happen unless he was brutally honest with her.

"You said you wanted to talk," she said. "So, talk."

He set his glass on the table and studied her face. Her cheeks were flushed, but her eyes were clear. "How much wine have you had?"

"Not so much that I can't tell you're stalling."

"No." He shook his head. "I'm not stalling. I just want to be sure you're clear-headed when I tell you everything."

"I'm finally going to get some answers?"

"Not some."

She frowned.

"All of them."

She looked up, eyes wide.

"I'm going to tell you everything. Answer every question. Fill in all the blanks."

"Really?" Her hand trembled, and she put her own glass down on the table.

"Really. There's just one thing before we start." Just in case it didn't go well, he needed one thing from her.

Her brow lifted, but she didn't frown or back away. "What?"

He pulled her into his arms and covered her mouth with his.

⁜

He tasted the wine on her lips, on her tongue. Thought he'd get drunk on it. On her.

She pulled back, and he met her gaze. Got lost in it.

This kiss was better than the last. Better than any of the ones before. This one said she trusted him, welcomed him, wanted him.

Damien was all too happy to oblige her desires, but this wasn't the time. He couldn't be with her again until she knew who he truly was and accepted him for it. God help him if she didn't.

"This doesn't sound like a wine conversation. How about I make us some coffee?"

"Okay by me." Okay? The last thing he needed was caffeine. Coward that he was, he grasped desperately at the delay. It was just what he needed to get his thoughts in order.

He scoffed to himself. Like that was even possible.

It was also the last time she'd look at him without seeing the monster inside.

He waited, the silence nearly unbearable, until the coffee was ready. After puttering around in the kitchen, she returned with a tray laden with cloth napkins, a carafe, two mugs, two spoons, a creamer, and a sugar bowl. He made his with a lot of cream and sugar. She took hers black, then settled back into the corner of the sofa again.

Damien chugged half of his, scalding his throat and not caring in the slightest. He was officially out of stall tactics and couldn't put off the talk any longer. "So, uh, do you want to ask questions, or do you just want me to start?"

"Why don't you start at the beginning, and if I have questions, I'll jump in."

"Okay." No, that wasn't okay. The most unbelievable part of his story was the beginning. It might be better to start somewhere else and circle back.

"Damien? I'm waiting."

"Sorry." He cleared his throat. "I was just trying to decide if that was the best course of action. It might be better to start with me fighting Ramer, but you'd need context, so the beginning would probably be best."

She frowned and put her mug down. "Are you stalling?"

"Honestly, no. Well, maybe. Yes. No."

Rina sighed. "Are you going to tell me what's going on or not?"

He ran his hand over his head, marveled that he'd only learned to turn human a short time ago yet he was already accustomed to his human head and not his horns.

"Maybe you should just go."

"Rina, wait."

She glared at him.

"I want to tell you. And I want to start at the beginning. But I'm only now realizing how ridiculous this story is. How unbelievable you'll find it."

"What if I promise not to say a word until you're done. That way you'll get the whole story out and we won't get sidetracked on a stupid detail."

He tilted his head and considered her. "You promise?"

"Yes." She sighed. "I promise. Now, start already, would you?"

Damien looked into her eyes, prayed it wasn't the last time they looked back at him with kindness, then he began.

✠

"What do you know about the Normandy Campaigns?" Damien asked.

"I'm a European History major," Rina said. "From 1200 to 1204, England and France battled for territories. England lost Normandy, Anjou, and Maine, but they kept Aquitaine."

"Yeah, I know a lot about the earlier battles. Less about the outcome."

"What does that have to do with anything?"

"Remember, no questions. Just let me get through this."

"You asked first," she muttered.

Damien sighed. "The crown was at stake. When Richard the Lionhearted died, two different factions claimed they were next for the throne."

"I know all this. But what—"

He held up his hand to silence her. "Nobles went to war. The battles were bloody. Knights who had previously fought with honor for righteous causes now found themselves engaging in war against prior allies, men they had battled with side-by-side in the Crusades. The toll that takes on a man..."

He shook his head and got lost in memories he'd suppressed centuries ago. Memories he knew could destroy him.

His voice was soft when he continued. "You can't understand the horrors of war unless you've been in it. The blood, the pain, and oh God, the stench. The muck of mud mingled with the coppery smell of death and the excrement of those who lay slain, trampled. Lifting your shield to deflect blows that seem to be coming from every direction. Lifting your weapon to strike down another, to take a life? Every bone in your body aches. Every muscle screams in agony with a step or a lunge, a blow or a block.

"Then it happens. You bend to extract the sword you'd plunged into another man's chest, and when you yank it out, the guy's helmet falls off. You see the shock and the horror etched on his face, and you know it must mirror your own. Because you knew him. You'd fought alongside him. And now you've killed him.

"Dumbfounded, sickened, you freeze. It's a fatal mistake. When the sword pierces your back, you have one everlasting moment of searing agony, then nothing. The battle noise diminishes, the pain dulls, your vision dims. You're left with nothing but prayers that shouldn't be answered."

"Damien, you're talking like you were there. You weren't." She reached for him, took his hand. "I know you were former military."

He looked up at her.

"You didn't have to say it. The way you carry yourself, the way you wear your hair cropped close, the way you study a room. Hell, the way you don't talk about your history. Combat is written all over you. But, Damien, war isn't like that anymore. I'm sure you've seen some horrific things, things I couldn't possibly understand. But shields and swords? You're projecting your pain into the past, and that can't be healthy. Maybe there's someone at the VA who can talk with you—"

"Rina, it isn't like that."

"Well, what is it like? Because I can't for the life of me see how a veteran with PTSD imagining thirteenth century wars is healthy. Nor do I see how it has anything to do with you and me and Ramer."

"It has to do with everything. I'm not—projecting, or whatever. I am that soldier."

She tipped her head to the side and studied him. He wasn't sure what she saw when she looked at him, but he saw pity and concern etched on her face.

"Damien—"

"I'm not crazy. I'm military, but not modern military. I was born in England in 1182."

Her eyes grew wide, and she blinked rapidly.

"I'm not crazy, Katarina. I fought in the Crusades. The Normandy Campaigns, too. I fought, then finally, I lost. But I didn't die that day, not in the traditional sense, because I prayed to God. I prayed for forgiveness for the slaughter I wrought on the battlefield, for the men I'd mowed down in the name of war who were actually my brothers-in-arms. I prayed I wouldn't be damned for my actions because I had believed I was doing the honorable thing but learned too late I wasn't. I kept thinking about what I'd do differently if I had another chance, kept wishing I'd found a good woman, settled down as a farmer, and had a houseful of babies. Kept wondering what was in store for me on the other side since I'd made so many wrong choices.

"Then he came to me, said my prayers were answered."

"Who? God?"

"No. His angel. Anael."

Rina shifted in her seat, moving ever-so-slightly away from him. "Let me get this straight. You believe you're a knight born centuries ago who was slain on the battlefield, prayed for second chance, and was granted immortality by one of God's angels."

He shook his head. "No, not exactly. I'm not immortal."

"You think you've been alive for centuries. After being run through with a sword."

"I don't think it. I know it."

"So, you can't die?"

"Of course I can. This life wasn't just granted to me. There are rules to the deal. For centuries, I thought of it as a curse. Recently, however, I've come to understand this is my second chance. You're my second chance."

"Me? What do I have to do with any of this?"

"The angel made me a deal. I could move on and accept my fate, but he wouldn't tell me if I was going to Heaven or hell. Or, he would give me a second chance on earth. A chance to do good, a chance to realize my dreams. I would exist indefinitely, as a protector of the people of this world. Then, at some point in my future, I'd find the woman of my dreams. The one I was supposed to be with. When that happened, I could claim her as my own, stop being a protector, and be human again."

"And you think I'm that woman?" She stood and walked to the other side of the room, creating a large and definite distance between them.

"I know you are. I fought it since the first moment I saw you, but it's obvious."

She turned away, waved her hands in the air. "Wait. Did you say 'Human again?' What does that even mean? You mean, non-immortal?"

"I told you. I'm not immortal. Not really. I'm a—" But he just couldn't say it.

Rina turned toward him, put her hands on her hips. "Oh, now you stop talking. You spin this fantastic tale, but you stop here? Just say it, whatever it is."

"I'm not immortal. I'm a gargoyle."

Eighteen

Rina blinked once. Again. Surely she didn't hear him correctly. "I'm sorry. You're a what?"

Damien sighed, rubbed his hands over his face. "A gargoyle."

A tiny laugh burbled up from deep inside her. "A gargoyle. Like those stone monsters at the top of buildings."

"Well, technically I'm a grotesque, as I don't have a water spout. But most people know my kind as gargoyles, so, yeah, you can call me a gargoyle. For the record, though, gargoyles aren't monsters. According to lore—according to Anael—we were created to protect the buildings we perch on as well as innocent people from encroaching evil."

"You're telling me that every—what'd you call it? Grotesque?"

He nodded.

"Every grotesque on top of a building is really a creature designed to protect people."

"No, not every statue. At least, I don't think so. I've actually only met a few others like me, and they were all in France. None of the ones in this city ever come to life. That I know of."

"Damien, you don't really believe this, do you?"

"It's the truth!"

"It's ridiculous."

He closed his eyes and took a deep breath. "That's my life."

"Damien, think about it. You supposedly made this deal in Europe. But you're here, in Pittsburgh, Pennsylvania. In the United States of America. An entire ocean away. Even if we accept your premise of a deal as true, it doesn't explain you being here."

"I was on a cathedral in France for centuries. At some point during the Industrial Revolution, I was retrieved from the cathedral and put on a ship. I spent weeks in a cargo hold, and when the ship docked here, I was transported to the Nathaniel Burton Mansion, where I spend every daylight hour on my plinth, watching people. At night, I'm free."

Rina walked into the kitchen. She heard Damien calling her from the living room, but he didn't follow, and for that, at least, she was grateful. Whiskey called to her. It was no longer late at night. It was early morning, but she didn't care. She took it out of the cabinet, thought about grabbing a glass, and instead drank straight from the bottle. The burn started in her throat and blazed a trail to her stomach, but the pain did nothing to clarify her thoughts.

He was insane. She'd slept with a clinically delusional man.

Then something occurred to her. Something that made her cringe, made rage burn through her hotter than the whiskey. She stormed back into the living room, bottle still in hand.

"You know, I admit, I haven't had much experience with relationships. The few I've had in my lifetime, I've somehow managed to make a mess of. I've broken up with men, and I've had a few break up with me. Sometimes things got pretty ugly. But never, and I mean *never*, in my entire life have I heard of anyone using a woman for sex and then telling a lie of this proportion to get out of the relationship. You must think I'm an absolute moron if you thought I'd believe this cockamamie story. If you want out, have the decency to tell me. But don't lie. And for the love of God, don't tell a lie so outrageous that you insult my intelligence."

"Rina, I don't want out. I'm telling you all this so we can move forward with nothing but the truth between us."

She stared at him for a moment, then she took another swig of whiskey. When nothing changed, she took another. The burn was less noticeable, but the ridiculousness of the situation was still perfectly clear.

She slammed the bottle down on the coffee table. "Fine. You want to stick by that story, stick by it."

"It's the only story I have."

"Well, if you want me to believe it, you're going to have to prove it to me."

"Prove it? How?"

"Turn back into stone."

"I don't control it like that. The sun comes up, and I petrify. It goes down, I'm released."

"I've never seen a gargoyle look like," she waved at him, "like you. Especially not on the roof of a mansion in Pittsburgh."

"This isn't my animated-creature form. This is my human form."

"Okay. You can't become stone. So turn into your creature form."

"Huh."

"What does that mean?"

"Well, this human thing is new to me. I never managed to change out of my creature form until I saw you. All of my changes are because of you."

"I prompted you to become human?"

"That's what Anael said."

"Anael?"

"My angel, remember?"

"He's still around?"

"He's always around. I'm one of his charges. He's the only entity I talked to for centuries."

"Except for those few grotesques in France."

"Right."

She pinched the bridge of her nose. "I see."

"Anyway, he said when I really wanted it, really needed to become human, I would. I never believed him. Gave up on it ever happening. Then that night, when Ramer first attacked you, I went after him. I assumed it would be as a gargoyle, but I didn't want to reveal myself, so I stuck to the shadows. Somehow, between seeing him attack you and me attacking him, I ended up human. It was my first transformation, and since then, I've been able to do it anytime I wanted or needed to."

"So what's the problem? Change back." She couldn't stop herself from challenging him, just so she could prove him wrong and finally move on. To hell with what Urbani said. When she was done with this nightmare, she was packing her bags. It was time to get out of the city and start fresh somewhere else.

"That's the thing. I don't know how to force the change when the form I'm in now is the one I want to be in."

"Well, isn't that convenient?" She sat on the sofa, crossed her arms. Glared at him.

"Wait! Don't give up on me. At least let me try."

She gestured for him to make the attempt.

He squinted. Pursed his lips. Clenched his fists.

"Nothing? I'm shocked."

"I'm trying. I feel the creature inside me, and I'm focused on the necessity of switching. But I just can't figure out how to do it. I think, on some primal level, I don't want you to witness it."

"As promised, I listened to your story. Now I think you should leave."

His head snapped up. "Uh-oh."

"Uh-oh, what?"

"Dawn's coming. I have to go." He turned for the door.

For some reason, his desire to leave—even though that's what she'd demanded of him—made her want him to stay. "Seriously?" She ran around him, blocking his way. "Now you've got some pretty strong motivation to change, right? Have to get back to your roof and all. Transform. Fly back."

His body quaked, sweat burst from him brow. "Time's almost up. Let me pass."

"Change."

"Rina, now. Let me go."

"That's what I figured. Nothing. You told this ridiculous lie, and now you're trying to use the sunrise as an excuse to leave. If you want me to believe you, change."

"Please." Sweat beaded on his brow.

"One of us is about to be proved right, and we both know it's me. When you don't transform, you'll be revealed as the liar we both know you are."

Damien trembled, looked at her with a longing she'd never seen before, then turned toward the window. The first rays of the sun peeked over the horizon and shone through her window.

When the light landed on him, he turned to stone.

Rina walked over to the contorted petrified form of Damien Stone. She knocked on his arm. All she accomplished was scraping her knuckles on the rough surface.

"Damien?" she whispered.

"He can hear you. He just can't respond."

Her shriek echoed off her apartment walls. She whirled

around to see who had spoken.

A large glowing man, dressed in a tunic, stood near her door. She reached for the bottle to use as a weapon, but the man raised his hands.

"Whoa. It's okay."

"A stranger in my house is not okay!"

"I'm not a stranger, Katarina. We know each other." The glow subsided, and she was able to better see the details of his face. Then his robes changed into a sweater and jeans.

The bottle slipped from her hands, spilled on the floor. "Al?"

He made a slight bow. "I can see you have questions."

Something between a chortle and a snort escaped her. "Questions? You can see I have questions. That's the understatement of the century. Or several centuries, I guess."

"I'll answer as many as I can. But first, I need to deal with Damien."

"Deal with him? He's a life-sized stone man in the middle of my living room. What can you possibly do with him?"

He looked down his nose at her. His tone, when he spoke, was laced with disdain. "Please. I'm an angel."

She watched, transfixed, as the stone man became a stone monster. Damien's short hair receded, horns popped out on his head. His teeth became fangs, and his clothes disappeared.

Al—or Anael—or whatever his name was flicked his wrist, then Damien disappeared entirely.

"Where'd he go?"

"Back to his plinth on Nathaniel Burton Mansion. We can't very well have a missing gargoyle on a highly traveled street in broad daylight, now, can we?"

Rina plopped onto the sofa. "This can't be happening. This can't be true."

He sat beside her, took her hand, held it between two of his. "Is it really so hard to believe? You've seen it with your own eyes."

"The whiskey. I must have had too much whiskey. That's it."

He strode across the room then rounded to face her. He still looked like a man, but wind whipped his hair and clothing, and his visage glowed again. His eyes blazed with the fire from a thousand suns. When he spoke, the deep timbre of his voice echoed through the apartment. "What is it with you humans? We ask you to take things on faith, and you can't. We show you proof, and you balk. Is nothing good enough? Is it really so difficult to believe in something? Anything?"

Rina cowered on the sofa. She was in the presence of a celestial being. A messenger of the Lord. And she'd angered him.

Anael closed his eyes. Soon his appearance reverted back to that of the human she knew to be Al DeAngelo.

Al. DeAngelo. Clever.

"I'm... I'm sorry. It's just, well, when you wake up in the morning, you don't expect to learn your boyfriend is a stone monster and his buddy is an angel. It's a lot to process."

He sat beside her again, and she made a conscious effort not to cringe away from him.

"Should I bow or something?" she asked.

He sighed. "I'm not the Lord, Katarina. I'm just here to help."

"There's so much I don't understand."

"I know. Let me try to explain." He conjured a cup of coffee and handed it to her.

She took a tentative sip. Sighed. Smiled. "This is delicious."

"Italian caffe from a little place in Rome. They roast the beans to perfection, and grind it fresh with a wheel, not a blade."

"You've ruined all other coffee for me."

"Katarina, I'm trying to make you more comfortable with this whole situation, but coffee will only go so far."

"I'm calm now. I'm ready to hear what you have to say."

"What Damien told you is all true."

"How do you know what he told me?"

"I can hear his thoughts. No matter where he is. I can hear him now."

"Now? What's he thinking?"

Anael sighed. "He's cursing the timing of the sun. Wondering how you're handling all of this. Wishing he'd explained better. Wondering if it wouldn't have been better for everyone if he had just died in battle. Everything you'd expect him to be thinking."

"I wish I could talk to him."

"Is there a message you wish me to convey?"

"You mean, you can talk to him when he's stone?"

"So could you. He can hear, see, feel. He just can't react."

"But he's not here."

"If I can read his thoughts from here, does it not stand to reason that I can impart your message from this same distance?"

She sipped her coffee. "This is just so new to me. So... remarkable."

"What would you have me tell him?"

"Nothing. Not yet. I need to hear more."

"Very well." He sat back, crossed one leg over the other. "Damien prayed for a second chance. One was granted to him. But with certain constraints, conditions, provisos, and the like."

"What are the terms of his deal?"

"In short, he was a knight. His job was to protect people. So, we made him a protector. For decades he acted in that capacity. His nightly sojourns were spent searching for evil-doers and protecting the innocent. But somewhere along the way, he stopped helping. Centuries passed without him giving humans a second thought."

"Why?"

"Why? Because he grew frustrated. He saw no end to it. Every day he was a statue, every night he was a warrior. But nothing ever changed. Evil kept coming. He never found his soul mate."

"Are you telling me God didn't know when and where his soul mate would be? That He couldn't conjure one for him?" Oh! Is that what had happened? Was she... conjured?

"You're getting ahead of yourself, Katarina."

"You can read my thoughts, too?"

"I can. Before you fret, know that is not something I do lightly. Or often. It's just making things easier at the moment."

"I don't like it. It's... a violation."

"Then you must be frank with me."

"So you'll stop?"

"For now."

She studied him for a moment before realizing how much she must have insulted him. Challenging an angel...

"If I might continue?"

Rina nodded.

"Damien was succumbing to despair in France. Despite what you think, angels are not privy to all things divine. God knew the time and place where Damien would find his mate, but I did not. To protect free will, the Lord keeps things even from His messengers. I saw Damien suffering but didn't know how to help him, so I took a chance and moved him here, hoping the change in scenery would give him the spark again. Unfortunately, he only grew more despondent. Eventually, he stopped trying."

"Didn't that void his deal?"

"No. Not exactly. It did cause me to worry that when his time was up, he wouldn't recognize the signs."

"The signs?"

"These deals aren't given to many people, and they're always based on a myriad of conditions—what kind of person he was in life, what potential he didn't fulfill, what his desires and fears were at the moment of death, and what he prayed for as he passed on. Part of his prayer was that he be given another chance to protect people. To do good in the world again. Realizing he'd caused so much pain to fellow warriors devastated him. When he didn't make it off that battlefield to begin to make up for that, it tore at him. That was why he was given a second chance, and that was why he was made a gargoyle. To try to atone."

"The people granted second chances? They aren't all gargoyles?"

"Their form is determined by many factors. Damien was a protector and wanted to continue protecting. Thus... a grotesque. Others have different forms, different rules."

"So, this became like a purgatory of sorts for him."

He shrugged. "From the human perspective, I suppose you could look at it that way."

"How does he get out of his purgatory?"

"That was the other part of the deal. He regretted not marrying, settling down. So we told him once he'd saved enough people, he'd get to meet his soul mate. Assuming he didn't mess anything up, he'd be made human again and granted a life with her."

"But he didn't protect enough people. You said he hadn't done his duty for years."

"Ah, but that wasn't truly the case. There is no set number. His... purgatory is actually self-defined. Once he realized he wasn't to blame for the atrocities he'd committed in service to his country, he'd be free. I couldn't tell him that. It's a lesson he had to learn on his own. I tried to encourage him to stay the course, but he'd grown too frustrated, too hopeless. If only he could have seen how close he'd gotten back in France. Instead, he hardened his thoughts, his heart. Moving him here didn't change that. And so he's waited and wasted all this time. Until now."

"I don't understand."

"It was you, Katarina. When he saw you, he had to help you. You thawed his heart, helped him sense his true mate, his potential future. And then he saved you. He began protecting again."

"Do you mean Ramer?"

He nodded.

"Was he intentionally put in my path?"

"I wouldn't manipulate things like that."

"Then what does he have to do with this?"

The angel shook his head and looked away. "I've already said too much."

Rina sighed. "Why didn't you just tell Damien all of this? Seems like you could have avoided so much trouble if you'd just been a little more forthcoming."

"I told you. He had to learn his lessons on his own. He'd been right on the cusp of it for so long, then he gave up. When you came into his life, he woke up. And he began to accept the truth of it all."

"What truth, exactly? I'm apparently the prize. I'd think I could be privy to this great realization."

He sighed. "You aren't a trophy, Katarina. Your feelings are your own. Your path is yours to choose."

"So, what's Damien's truth, if not me?"

"I told you. His truth was that he did nothing wrong. He looked at his time in battle as a compilation of sins. Murder after murder. Sinful carnage and bloodletting. When he went to rescue you, he finally learned there is a difference between cold-blooded killing and the tragedies of war."

"And how did he learn that just by rescuing me?"

"Because the feelings he had for Ramer and the feelings he had in battle were two very different things. When he saw Ramer attack you, he wanted to kill him."

Her stomach flopped. "He's homicidal?"

"No. Not at all. He didn't kill Dylan Ramer. He just acknowledged the difference in feelings. War was passionate but clinical. In its own violent way, honorable. And Damien is nothing if not a man of honor. That was why this was so hard for him. Only when he saw the result of battle up close, when he saw he'd slain a former friend, did his actions overwhelm him with guilt. However, he eventually learned that, while God doesn't want His children to kill, He understands casualties of war. Read the Good Book. There are wars all through it. Peace will eventually come. In the meantime, soldiers can't be faulted for doing their jobs."

"But Ramer?"

"Ramer he also felt passionately about. But that wasn't war. That was vengeance. Damien brought his feelings under control. He now knows the difference."

"Did he finally just get it, or was it because it was me?"

"Does it matter?" Anael asked. "He learned his truth, and he found his soul mate."

"I'm just supposed to take all this on faith and be with him?"

"Do you love him?"

"I—I don't know. I haven't known him very long. Now I learn I didn't really know him at all. It's kind of hard to commit to a life with him before processing all this."

"Once Damien rises this evening, you two should talk." He rose.

"Wait. Don't go."

"Is there something more?"

"Well, yeah. There's a lot more. What happens to Damien if I say no?"

"He'll have to continue on his search for a mate. He is still due the second part of his contract, and we keep our promises."

"What happens if he makes the choice to walk away from me?"

"He knows the terms of his deal, Katarina. You can't let that sway *your* decision."

"It leaves me unsettled."

"Why?"

"I've felt him pull away. I didn't know why—I still don't —but I'm not sure he's committed to me yet."

Anael sat again. "He pulled away because he didn't feel good enough for you. Now he knows he is. He worried he had nothing to offer you. He has been observing life for centuries, but he's hardly lived it. He didn't know how he would care for you, provide for you."

"Now he does? I don't see how anything has changed."

"No, now he doesn't care. If you accept him, he's determined to figure it all out, but he's concluded he doesn't need to have those answers to profess his love. That's why he came to you and told you his story. He's finally ready to take a leap of faith. If you aren't, if you don't accept him, he'll remain as he is. I assume he'll make a stronger effort to learn the ways of this world, though, so he's better prepared the next time."

"But he's right. He doesn't know technology. This world must be foreign to him. I mean, how will we live? He doesn't even have a social security number. How will he get a job? He has no record of ever having been born. No digital footprint. How can we explain all that away?"

"Is it important to you that he provide for you?"

"No. I can always make money somehow. I worry about his feelings. He's from a time where the man provided. I don't want him to feel emasculated. Then there's societal pressure. People will question him about where he came from, what he does for a living. When he can't answer, what will happen to him? I just want him to be safe."

Anael gestured to himself. "Hello. Angel? I can provide him with whatever he needs."

Rina bit her lip, thought these things through. If Anael could simplify the logistics of it all, could she make a life with Damien? She thought of the lengths he'd gone to protect her. Thought of the way he virtually worshipped her in the bedroom and out. Thought of the anguish on his face when he turned to stone. Probably thought he'd lost her for good.

She wasn't ready for a ring on her finger, but she could see a future with him. It would be good. So good.

"Please send word to him not to worry. I understand and believe. Let him know I'll be waiting for him this evening."

Anael nodded. "Done."

Something had been bothering her, some feeling she ignored when she tried to process all this information. Now that Anael had explained everything, that 'something' became clear.

"Anael. One more thing."

"Yes?"

"Who is Pino?"

The angel sighed. "His real name is Penemuel. He's my brother."

"So that much was true. He's your angelic brother."

"Well, he's my brother. He's not angelic, however."

"How can that be?"

"He's fallen."

Pinpricks of cold danced through her nerve endings, giving her a chill. "What? A fallen angel? Why is he here? What does he want from me?"

"He's here to balance the scales. I broke the rules by helping Damien too much. He's here to turn things back toward a more neutral bent."

"By dating me?"

"He can't overtly harm you. But he can cause chaos. I'd suggest you keep your distance."

"But now you've appeared to me, told me all about Damien. Won't Pino need to balance the scales again?"

Anael didn't answer her. He frowned, and then he was gone.

It was going to be a long day.

Nineteen

Damien spent all day thinking at Anael. Unfortunately, he didn't answer much while he was talking to Rina. As soon as the angel left her, he appeared on the roof. Damien bombarded him with questions and didn't wait for answers, so the angel disappeared and remained silent.

It didn't stop Damien from think-yelling at him, though.

When the last rays of the sun disappeared behind the horizon, Damien came to life with a roar. As soon as the stone morphed into flesh, he stretched his wings, squatted, and prepared to fly away.

A soft squeak stopped him.

He whirled around to find Rina standing there.

"Katarina? What are you doing here?"

"Al brought me."

"It's not safe. You might fall."

"He said you'd see me down safely."

"Stay there. I'll come to you." Damien stepped off his plinth and headed toward her. His claws dug into the roof, making a loud scraping noise with each footfall. He paused, looked down at himself. Shame and disgust roiled through him.

Was a blush noticeable when he was in creature form?

When he stopped approaching Rina, she started walking toward him. His head snapped up, but too late. She'd slid on the loose grit of the roof and lost her footing. Her fall was both too slow and too fast. Damien didn't even think. He flapped his wings and soared to her, clutching her just before she toppled over the edge.

She squealed when he grabbed her. Was it fear? Relief? He didn't know. All he knew was that he had to get her to safety.

He flew to the top of Mount Washington and set her down carefully, hidden in a copse of trees. "Are you all right?"

She flung her arms around him. "Thank you."

Damien started to hug her, then dropped his arms and stepped back from her.

"What's wrong? Where are you going?"

"I'm going to transform, but I need more space. I might thrash, and I don't want to hurt you."

Rina approached him and reached up to cup his cheek. She smiled at him. "I don't mind how you look."

He turned away. "I'm hideous."

She pulled his head back to face her, traced the ridges on his head and his horns with both hands. "I think this is the most heroic thing I've ever seen. It's glorious."

He looked down at her, blinked a few times. His mind wasn't playing tricks on him. She was smiling—not laughing at him, but smiling—and completely serious.

She must be crazy.

He pulled away, got a safe distance from her, then began to transform into his human form. This time, when his skeleton resized and his tissue regenerated, he fought to control the change, the pain.

It took a little longer, but it hurt less.

A few deep breaths, then he was over the worst of it. He looked at Rina.

She approached him. "You didn't have to do that for me."

"I can't very well walk around with wings and a tail."

She smirked. "No, I suppose not. But I meant what I said. I didn't mind."

He took her hand and led her out of the trees. They approached a railing that protected pedestrians on the over-look from falling down the mountain. "Why were you on the roof?"

"I told you. Al brought me."

"Yes, but why?"

"We weren't done talking."

Damien rubbed his head. He was used to human features now but still surprised to find his short hair so soft under his palm.

If only his other form weren't so... rough.

He went to take her hand then reconsidered. "We can stand here and admire the view, or we can go somewhere and finish our discussion."

"I have to work tonight, so I don't have much time. The view is spectacular, though."

"So, postpone the talk and enjoy the view?" Damien scanned the cityscape below them. The moonlight reflected off the rivers, the bridges that spanned them alive with red and white lights from the vehicles speeding over them. The build-ings beyond, shadowed monoliths stretching toward the sky, bore thousands of lit windows, mimicking the stars above it. It really was a beautiful sight.

She followed his gaze. "The view is nice from up here, but it's even nicer from up there."

"Up where? This is the highest point in the city."

"Wow, you're thick. I mean up there." Rina pointed toward the sky.

"You liked flying?"

"I loved it. I never felt so free, so alive. I could do it forever."

"I've done it nearly forever. Trust me, it loses its allure after a while."

"Really? I thought it was fun."

She wasn't wrong. It could be fun, but more often than not, it was a reminder to him of his supernatural prison. Unsure how to answer her, he just shrugged.

"Well, I don't know how it is to fly for centuries. Maybe it's no different than the wonder of walking—fun when we first learn and then just a matter of fact. But flying is new to me, so I find it exhilarating. What do you say? Take the quick way back to my apartment?"

He frowned at her.

"I'm sorry. Maybe it hurts too much to turn back. Forget I asked. Want to take the incline down, or should I call a cab?"

He'd never been on an incline, nor had he been in a vehicle. While both options intrigued him, he didn't know how much either would cost. He wasn't even certain he would comprehend the values of the money Anael provided in his wallet. It had taken him what felt like forever to count out bills to pay for their snack at the restaurant in Oakland.

For that matter, was the angel even allowed to provide him with money? Maybe that was another rule Anael broke. Maybe Damien's wallet was now empty.

All that aside, she'd struck a blow to his ego. He couldn't abide her worrying about his pain. He'd endure endless torture for her. A tiny transformation didn't concern him.

If only he didn't have to look like a monster to appease her.

"You do know what inclines and cabs are, right?"

"Yes, I know what inclines and cabs are. I've lived here longer than you, remember?"

"Have you ever ridden in either?"

He set his jaw and crossed his arms.

"I guess living here for decades doesn't make you an expert in everything, does it?"

She had him there.

"Okay," she said. "How about we make it a four-fer? We'll take the incline down to Station Square, the subway through the city as far as it runs, hop on a bus to my apartment, then after I'm ready, a cab to Bar Belles."

"You sure you don't want to hop on the Gateway Clipper, too? Throw a boat ride into the mix?"

"Someone's touchy. Come on, let's go get tickets for the incline." She held her hand out to him.

Instead of taking it, he stepped back, looked around, and seeing no one, willed himself to transform again. Even before he'd finished the change, he managed to focus on Rina. Saw the initial fear in her eyes before she could mask her expression. She'd never accept him. Not fully. He gave her credit for trying, but he couldn't force her to embrace the monster inside him.

Or maybe he was just angry because in reality, he was a monster with a human inside him.

The frustration built inside him until he couldn't stand the stress. He let out a loud roar, and she cringed.

"Sorry," he muttered. "Just had some pent-up energy to expel."

"I didn't mind," she said.

To his knowledge, that was the first time she lied to him. It crushed both his human and monster halves.

He didn't say another word, merely scooped her up then sprang into the air. She squealed and giggled, and her reaction seemed genuine. But that didn't surprise him. Flying was fun. Even all these centuries later, sometimes he enjoyed nothing more than a soar through the clouds.

Other times, it was just one more reminder that he wasn't human anymore.

Fuck it. If this was the last time he would fly with her, he'd make it a flight to remember.

He beat his wings to gain speed and took her into the first cloud he saw. The mist was cool, damp, and utterly refreshing. Once through the clouds, he took her high into the sky where the stars and moon shone bigger, brighter. He soared there until he felt goosebumps on her flesh. She didn't have his protective skin, and the height and the damp made her cold. So he held her tighter to share his body heat, then he flipped and dove toward the earth, spinning like a corkscrew until even he grew dizzy. Her shrieks carried to him on the wind, and he pulled up right above the Monongahela, skimming her along the river. She reached down to touch the water and laughed when it splashed them. One final time he ascended, flew over the tallest buildings in the city, then headed to her apartment where he landed on her fire escape beside her broken window.

"That was amazing!"

Her bright eyes and flushed skin pleased him. He'd given her a memory to cherish. That was all he could offer, and it delighted him to know he'd at least been successful at that.

"Come inside, keep me company while I get ready." She lifted the plastic sheeting and climbed inside.

He stared at the flapping film and worried over her safety. That window had been broken for far too long, and he knew that was how Ramer got in. If only he knew how to fix it, then he could do something helpful for her. Something more important and vital than providing a pleasurable memory.

Getting inside with his wings was difficult, so he transformed before stepping inside. He blinked, his human eyes needing a moment to adjust from the darkness outside to the lamplight in her bedroom. When his vision cleared, he saw Rina had already stripped out of her jeans and sweater. He averted his eyes.

No point in starting something they didn't have time to finish.

No point, period, since he had to leave her.

"I thought we were going to talk for a bit."

He couldn't bear to look at her. His voice cracked, and he cleared his throat. "There's really not much time. We'll have to talk later."

"Later, then. Maybe you can come to the club. Walk me home after?"

"Sure. I'll be there before closing."

"Why not just spend the evening there? Keep me company if we aren't swamped?"

"You know, most women wouldn't want men to go to a club like that."

"I'm not worried. You never seem to take in the show when you're there."

Wasn't that the truth? He only had eyes for her.

"Are you ready? I can walk you there."

She pouted. "Not going to fly me?"

"Too crowded over there this early. Someone might notice."

"Okay." She shrugged. "The boring way, then."

Yet another difference between them. He loved being able to walk without scrutiny. Something she took for granted but he relished.

That, and he never found a moment they spent together boring.

As Damien expected, the club was busy all night. Rina wouldn't be able to visit him. He'd be alone for hours with nothing but his thoughts to occupy him.

They made for poor company.

He sat in a dark corner and tried to be unobtrusive, but

Rina saw him. She walked over with a full tray and put a mug of beer on his table.

"You can't stay without purchasing something. I'd rather you not buy a lap dance, so drink whatever you'd like. My treat."

He nursed the beer she brought him and glared at the golden liquid. She thought he couldn't afford one lousy beer, let alone a night full of them.

As he still hadn't looked in his wallet, he didn't know whether she was right. Even if he did have money, he hadn't earned it. So, in that regard, she was spot on.

It would rankle any man, but a man from the thirteenth century? It was embarrassing. Intolerable. Unacceptable.

It was also another reason he wasn't right for her.

He sighed and looked around the club. The dancers didn't interest him. Tiny and Gretchen made time to glare at him, but neither approached his table. Rina was the only person in the club who captured his attention, and she could barely spare him a smile let alone a moment to chat.

With nothing to do, he continued sipping his beer and tried to tamp down his humiliation.

It didn't work. Only proved his earlier conclusion to be true.

Damien scanned the crowd for about the twentieth time that night. No sign of Ramer, which was good. But something didn't sit right with him. He had a niggling feeling that something was coming, something bad. All his senses tingled like they had before battles, but he didn't see any imminent threat.

As the night wore on, the feeling only grew worse.

He called out to Anael, but the angel didn't show. He tried talking about his concerns mind-to-mind but received no answer.

Maybe danger wasn't on the horizon. Maybe he just dreaded the talk he had to have with Rina.

He looked across the club and met her gaze. Even deep in

thought he'd managed to track her every move, find her easily through the crowd. She smiled a dazzling smile at him, one he could only half-heartedly return.

Their differences spanned more than their species. If he chose her as his destiny, he'd become human—but not the human she deserved. He carried too much baggage. There were too many centuries between them. Too much carnage. It had taken him a long time to realize his actions on the battle-field were not murderous, but in service to his country and his God.

It had only taken him a moment longer to realize that, regardless of his motives, he had too much blood on his hands to deserve Katarina.

There were too many ways he didn't fit into her world, and he'd never be able to assimilate. Not in her lifetime, anyway. He should have paid closer attention through the centuries. Now he'd learned his lesson, but he learned it too late. Maybe, with an extraordinary amount of contrition, he could be given a third chance down the road. A last chance to embrace humanity, to find another soul mate.

Who was he kidding? He didn't want another soul mate.

He was damned.

The club grew emptier and emptier, and Damien wallowed deeper and deeper into self-pity. He ignored the feeling eating away at his gut and tried to drown his sorrows in beer after beer.

Beer that Rina had paid for.

It had been centuries since he'd imbibed so much, and he felt the effects. The room spun a bit, and he was only too glad when the last patron left, the flashing lights subsided, and the music stopped

He watched while tables were wiped, chairs were flipped, and floors were scrubbed. The bartender counted money then left. The dancers, one by one, emerged from their dressing room then walked out the back door, each accompanied by a member of the security staff. Soon only Tiny, Gretchen, and Rina were left, and they engaged in a heated discussion before Rina walked away from them. They both glared at Damien—again—before walking out the back.

"I'm just going to lock up back there," Rina called to him. She disappeared for a moment, then returned to the main room. Her shoes dangled from her left hand, her purse was slung over her right shoulder.

"You ready?" He dreaded them leaving and having the conversation he'd been putting off, but he also knew he was out of time.

"Let's just stay here. I can make us some appetizers, if you're hungry."

The thought of human food appealed to him—must have been because of the beer—and his stomach growled.

"What do you like? Chicken wings? Jalapeño poppers? Cheese sticks? Nachos—Do you even know what those things are?"

"Yes." Well, some of them, anyway.

She turned toward the kitchen, but he grabbed her hand. He didn't want her serving him after she'd served the crowd all night.

"Sit. I'm fine."

"Your stomach growled. You must be hungry."

"Sit." He pulled on her hand until she plopped onto the bench, tossed her bag and shoes on the table, then slid over beside him. He patted his lap. "Put your feet up."

"What?"

"I know your feet hurt. You took off your shoes, and you're limping a little. Let me rub your feet."

Her brow raised, and she sat still for a moment. Then she shrugged and lifted her feet onto his thighs.

She had such dainty feet, such tiny toes. Though the hosiery he could see the nails were painted a deep red, the same color as her fingernails.

"Mmmm." She closed her eyes and lay down in the booth. "That feels heavenly."

He continued to rub her toes, her arches, her heels. Soon her breaths grew deep and regular, and he knew she slept.

They had much to discuss, but she looked so peaceful. She needed her sleep. Instead of waking her, he let her rest.

A few hours passed, and he simply sat and watched over her. The number of chances he had to just hold her had dwindled to one, and he planned on savoring it.

Her phone rang, and he reached for her bag, hoped to silence it before it woke her.

But she woke anyway.

"Sorry," he said. "I tried to find it and turn it off."

She dug in her bag. "That's okay. It was rude of me to—" She swiped her finger across the screen and answered the call. "Hello?"

He couldn't hear the other end of the call, but he didn't like what he saw. Color drained from Rina's face, and she clenched the phone tighter. "I'm coming right now."

"What's wrong?" Damien asked.

"That was Gretchen. Ramer attacked her."

Damien flew Rina to Gretchen's in a matter of seconds. He landed them behind her building, transformed again, then escorted her around front.

Two police cars, an ambulance, and an SUV were parked on the street.

"Bet that's Detective Urbani's car," she said.

He thought the same thing.

They rushed inside and up to Gretchen's apartment.

"Whoa." An officer stood outside her door and blocked their path.

"It's okay," a man's voice called from inside. "Let them in."

Detective Urbani stood in the middle of the room, blocking Damien's view of Gretchen. Rina dashed inside. He followed, stopping short when Urbani stepped out of the way.

"Oh, my God!" Rina rushed over to her friend, sat beside her, and took her hand.

Damien didn't know what to say. Both of Gretchen's eyes were swollen almost completely shut. She had a split lip, bruises on her neck, and a sling supporting her arm. Two medical workers tended her, bandaging cuts and monitoring vital signs.

Damien was angry she'd been the victim of such a violent assault, but at the same time grateful it wasn't Rina.

"You need to go to the hospital," Rina told her.

Gretchen shook her head slowly, grimaced, then hissed in a deep breath.

"Oh, Gretch."

"I didn't tell him," she mumbled.

"Tell him what?" Rina asked. "What did he want? Why did he do this?"

She took a jittery breath. "Wanted you. Said you weren't home. Said I had to know where you were. Said he'd beat it out of me. But I didn't tell."

"You should have. I was safe with Damien. Look what he did to you."

"Just so... you're safe." She took another quivering breath. "He wanted to kill me. Would have... if cops didn't come."

"How'd you know to come?" Damien asked Urbani.

"A neighbor heard the ruckus and called. Lucky we had a car in the area."

"How'd Ramer escape?"

Urbani looked around the room. "Must have heard the sirens and got out."

Rina jumped to her feet and rounded on the detective.

"Do you see what happened? Do you believe us now? How can you possibly twist things so this is our fault, or so we did it to cover our tracks?"

Urbani scanned the room. "Officers, you can go back on patrol." The uniformed policemen left the room. "Miss Kiebler, do you require any further assistance from the EMTs?"

"No," Gretchen whispered.

"Go ahead," he said to the man and woman assisting her. "You can go."

The female paramedic said, "Miss, you really should go to the hospital. If you don't want to go in the ambulance, at least have your friend take you."

"Thanks, but I'll be fine." Gretchen's words came out slurred.

The male attendant packed up a bag, and the woman mouthed something at Rina. Probably telling her to talk some sense into her friend. Given the little Damien knew about Gretchen, he didn't think she'd give in.

After everyone left, Urbani closed the door. He walked back into the room, and spoke to Rina in a low voice. "I thought you understood after I visited you in your home."

"Understood what?"

He put his finger to his lips and inclined his head toward the hall.

Could someone really be there listening? It made sense. He'd cleared the room at Rina's, too, before he said anything. But Damien couldn't remember him saying anything that would have prevented this.

"I guess I was too subtle." He sat on the coffee table, facing the girls, then leaned closer so they could hear his whispered words. "Dylan Ramer is protected. Up until now, it was his word against yours. No one with half a brain would take his side, but I had to pretend to be on the fence because I'm also being watched. The best way I could help you was to pretend not to believe you. Now that Ramer's escalated, it's going to be harder for him to spin a yarn about what happened. Harder, but not impossible. There's a camera in the vestibule, but footage can always be erased or lost. And your bouncer friend, Tiny? He's the likely choice for Ramer to try to pin this on. Hopefully he has an air-tight alibi. Or you." He turned toward Damien. "Do you have an alibi for tonight?"

"Wait a minute." Rina waved her hands in the air.

Urbani held a finger to his lips.

"What are you talking about?" Her tone was quieter, but it hadn't softened. "Why do Damien and Tiny need an alibi? Gretchen told you what happened. And who is protecting Ramer? Why is he even after us?"

Damien finally understood. It made sense now... Urbani being careful about what he disclosed and when he disclosed it, and Ramer successfully deflecting blame, avoiding arrest.

"Do you still not see?" Urbani said.

Damien fought to hold in a growl. "When you said he was protected, I thought you meant on the crime side. Powerful lawyers and lots of intimidation tactics. But you mean on the legal side. He's got someone on your force looking out for him."

Everyone—even Gretchen—turned and looked at him.

"Exactly," Urbani said.

"How'd you figure that out?" Rina asked.

He shrugged. "Just makes sense."

She scowled and turned back toward Urbani. "Can't you report the dirty cop to your superior?"

"Maybe you don't get it." The detective sighed and shook his head. "The dirty cop *is* my superior."

⁂

Damien had never felt so helpless. Gretchen refused to go to the hospital, and despite Rina's request, Urbani couldn't even provide an officer to watch Gretchen's place until morning. He left shortly after he dropped his bombshell.

"I think I should stay with her overnight," Rina said. "Our talk will have to wait."

"I don't think you should stay here," Damien said. "Ramer could come back."

"Well, I can't take her home with me. Ramer not only knows where I live, he has an open window to climb right in."

So that's what a metaphorical knife to the heart felt like. He didn't even have a safe haven for her. What would they do? Spend the day perched on his roof while waiting for him to wake up?

"What about a hotel?"

"I don't have the money for that."

No time like the present. He took his wallet out and opened it. There were several bills in there and a few plastic cards. "Will any of this work?"

She furrowed her brow. "Where'd you get money? And a credit card?"

"Anael said I'd need a way to blend in, so he provided it to me. I'm not sure, but I think it got him in trouble."

"Then we probably should use it."

"The damage is done, Rina. Besides," he looked away, lowered his voice, "it's all I can offer you. I can't take you to my... home. This is the least I can do."

"Oh, Damien, I didn't mean to—"

Gretchen moaned, cutting her off.

"Take what you need." He pushed his wallet toward her. "Enough for a cab, a room at a nice place, and food."

She bit her lip. He could tell she was torn between saving her friend and explaining herself to him. But it was unnecessary. He knew the intent behind her words, knew she didn't mean to hurt his feelings. It wasn't her fault he couldn't do more, couldn't provide on his own.

Just another way he didn't belong in her life.

He offered the wallet again. "Please, Rina. Take it. I have to leave. I can feel dawn approaching. I have less than an hour. I suspect I don't have enough time to see you two safely to a hotel. This is all I can do."

She took his wallet, slipped one card and a few bills out of it, then handed it back. "I only took the card in case of emergency. And no matter how much I spend, I'll pay you back."

"That's not necessary."

"I don't want to get Al in trouble. More trouble."

He shook his head. "Whatever gets you moving. Let's go."

She called a cab company, then she gathered a few things for Gretchen, who had fallen asleep on the couch. When Rina came out of the bedroom, she frowned. "I hate to wake her."

"I'll carry her. Are you ready?"

She nodded and walked to the door.

Damien gently lifted Gretchen into his arms and walked out of the apartment. He carried her down the stairs, Rina right in front of him. When they got outside, Damien looked around. The eastern horizon was already turning a pearly gray.

"Just put her down," Rina said. "I know you have to go."

Damien set Gretchen down on the sidewalk and leaned her against her building.

"I should probably start waking her," Rina said. "I won't be able to carry her into the cab, anyway."

"Let her sleep," a voice from the shadows said. "I'll get to her soon enough."

Damien spun around. Ramer stood there, sneer on his face.

"Ramer." Damien pushed Rina behind him. A growl rumbled from deep inside him, and he felt the pull of his creature form. He wanted to claw Ramer's eyes out, rip him to bloody threads. Red tinged his vision, and he struggled for control.

"What do you want from me?" Rina peered out from behind Damien's shoulder.

"What do I want? You witnessed one of my drug deals. My associates can't afford loose ends. They dispatched me to tie them up. That means you. And your battered friend there."

"We didn't witness anything!"

"Doesn't matter one way or the other, now. I've toyed with you for too long. I thought we'd have time for more entertaining pursuits before I cleaned up this mess, but your henchman keeps foiling me at every turn. And speaking of your boyfriend, he's another loose end I need to take care of." He raised a gun, pointed it at Damien, and sneered.

"Wait!" Rina said. "I told you. I didn't witness anything. None of us did. Just go about your business. We won't even press assault charges. We can all walk away from this."

"I don't think so. My mistake was trying to enjoy you before ending you. But I can get a piece of ass anywhere, anytime, and far better than you. I won't make that mistake again. First your boyfriend, then your girlfriend, then you."

"Freeze!" Urbani stepped out from the shadowy side of the building, gun trained on Ramer.

Ramer turned sideways, kept his gun trained on Damien. With his free hand, he pushed a lock of greasy hair out of his eyes. "Detective, I'm sure you've heard from your boss that I'm off limits. Walk away, and I won't tell him how you inconvenienced me."

"Not this time. I've caught you in the act."

"I'll shoot him," Ramer said.

Damien trembled. He was almost out of time, and this standoff threatened to go on long after dawn broke.

"I'll kill every last one of them." Ramer's gun hand shook.

"Not before I drop you."

He turned his body, and his gun, toward the detective. "Then I'll start with you."

It was just enough to give Damien a chance. He charged at Ramer, tackling him to the ground. A shot rang out—Damien had no idea who fired or where the bullet went—and he prayed no one got hurt.

Rina screamed.

Ice cold panic sluiced through his veins.

He looked down into Ramer's sneering face. The sun crested the horizon.

Damien turned to stone.

Twenty

Rina didn't know what to do. Gretchen had come to and was screaming. Urbani still had his gun out, but it trembled in his hand.

No wonder. Damien had transformed, and now a massive statue lay on a bleeding Dylan Ramer.

"Get. This. Thing. Off." Ramer coughed. The spot of blood on the ground grew.

The cab pulled up. The driver took one look at the motley crew in front of him and floored it, leaving tire tracks behind him.

"What... What?" Urbani stuttered. Kept repeating the same word over and over.

Rina crossed to him, tried to lower his gun. It was like he had petrified, too. She couldn't push his arms down.

The sun grew brighter, and the first stirrings of life began in the city. The occasional car drove across a side street, and apartment lights turned on as the streetlights turned off.

"Detective? Detective!"

But he continued to babble.

She did the only thing she could think to do. She called for Anael.

To her surprise, both he and Penemuel showed up.

"Well," Penemuel said, "your boy here has made quite a mess of things, hasn't he?"

"Penemuel, that's not helping anything." Anael walked over to Gretchen and touched her forehead. She immediately fell back asleep. Then he touched the detective's forehead, and his trembling ceased. He lowered his gun and holstered it.

"Al," Rina said, "he waited too long. Can you help?"

"Isn't the first rule of this deal that he not reveal himself to any humans?" Penemuel asked.

She glared at him. How had she ever found him attractive? He was an ugly, reprehensible man.

"No," Anael said. "Actually, the most important rule is for him to be a guardian. A protector. A champion for good people and a warrior against evil. Given the current situation, I'd say he did a wonderful job of that." He snapped his fingers.

Damien disappeared.

"That's cheating." Penemuel twirled a pen in his hand, pocketed it, then scrutinized them.

"He's my charge, not yours. I'll deal with him however I see fit."

The fallen shrugged.

Rina stepped away from him, fear skittering up her spine. Anael had warned her about him. He could cause them more trouble than Ramer did.

"Anael. What are we going to do?" Rina's voice rose with each syllable, as did her stress. Her heart pounded in her ears, almost deafening her.

"For one thing, stop being so obvious that you're talking to us. No one else can see us."

"Not even them?" She gestured to the detective and Gretchen.

"Not even them. They've seen one supernatural being today. They don't need to see us, too. So, please, lower your voice."

She nodded.

"Tell the detective to call in the injury." He looked around. "Too much time has passed already."

Rina walked over to Urbani. "Detective. *Detective.*"

He didn't respond, so she slapped him across the face.

After blinking a few times, he looked at her.

"Can you call this in? Call an ambulance for him."

"I shot him."

"Who cares? He's *dying*. Call someone."

He shook his head as if to clear his thoughts, then he retrieved his cell phone from his pocket. His call connected almost immediately. "This is Detective Stephan Urbani, badge number—"

Rina tuned him out and walked over to Anael, who had stepped away from Ramer. "Can you manipulate their memories? Make them forget what they saw?"

"We can," Anael said.

"But we won't," Penemuel said.

"But... but they saw Damien change."

"Damien knew the risks when he accepted his deal. Now he can accept the consequences of his actions."

"But that was hundreds of years ago! Before cell phone cameras and motor vehicles, and... and guns."

"Rina," the fallen said, "for a human, you aren't half bad. But you don't get it. We don't serve you."

She stamped her foot. "I thought God elevated people above angels."

His face darkened, and she got a glimpse of the evil within him. She didn't want to show her fear but couldn't hide it, recoiling and staggering backward.

Anael put his arm around her. "No need for a philosophical debate at the moment. I'll make sure Damien comes to you at nightfall. You should be safe now."

"But what about Damien's exposure?"

"That's a human problem," Penemuel said. Then he and Anael disappeared.

Rina paced in the waiting room at the hospital. She'd had far too much coffee to sit still, and far too much stress to relax. Ramer was in surgery, Gretchen was getting checked out, and Urbani was giving a statement to someone.

Only she didn't have something to do. So, she paced.

When Gretchen was released, a nurse wheeled her to the waiting room. Rina ran over to her and hugged her.

"Are you okay?" She helped Gretchen stand, then the nurse wheeled away the chair.

"They gave me a bunch of prescriptions." She lifted her hand and jiggled some papers. "And a shot of something. Nothing hurts right now."

"Good. That's good."

"I must have hit my head, though. My memories are all jumbled, and I had some hallucinations."

"Do you have a concussion?"

"No, but my head hurts, and I just can't make sense of what happened."

Guilt churned the acid in Rina's stomach. She wanted to set her friend's mind at ease, but maintaining the ruse helped Damien, so she didn't say anything. Instead, she hugged her again.

"I think I'd like to go home," Gretchen said.

"I'd go with you, but I want to know what happens to Ramer."

"So, that part was true?"

Rina nodded. She hoped Gretchen only remembered the shooting and not the stone statue falling on Ramer.

Gretchen's brow furrowed, and she rubbed her head. "I'll wait, then."

"No, don't be silly. I'll call you a cab."

"I don't want you to have to sit here yourself."

"Detective Urbani is here. I won't be alone much longer. I'm sure he'll be done giving his statement soon."

"Where's Damien?"

How she hated lying to her friend. "Don't you remember? He left your apartment right before you fell asleep."

"He did? I don't remember..." She shrugged. "I guess I really hit my head hard."

Rina swallowed. "That's what you said."

Gretchen looked like she was going to ask a question, and Rina didn't want to lie anymore, so she busied herself with her phone, calling for a cab. She was told one was out front dropping someone off, and dispatch would have the driver wait for them.

"Come on. Your ride's here."

"That was fast," Gretchen said. "Or did I black out again?"

Rina's stomach flopped. "Poor baby. No, you didn't black out. But you definitely need to go home and rest."

She assisted Gretchen out to the cab then went back inside.

Urbani was waiting for her. "We need to talk," he said.

Of course they needed to talk. But what the hell could she possibly say?

He led her over to a bank of seats in quiet corner. She crossed her legs and bounced her foot.

Urbani reached over and put his hand on her knee to still the movement. "I know what I saw."

"And what exactly was that?" she asked.

"I saw your boyfriend tackle Ramer just as I fired my gun."

"Yeah, I saw that, too."

"And did you also see him turn to stone when he landed? Then disappear into thin air?"

She felt the blood drain from her face and swallowed. Hard. "Detective, people don't turn into stone and vanish."

"So, what did I see?"

"I—" Didn't matter how long she'd been alone in the waiting room. She still had no answer to that question. "I don't know what you saw."

"Where'd Mr. Stone go?"

She cringed. Mr. Stone. It was so obvious, now that she knew. Could Urbani recognize the wordplay? Would she be able to redirect his attention?

"I think the blood all over him freaked him out. He ran."

Her best lie was to paint Damien as a coward? She hated herself.

"You expect me to believe a little blood bothered him? He has the bearings of a military man. I find that highly unlikely."

She shrugged. "What happens now?"

He sat back in his seat. "Now? Internal Affairs is off as we speak to take my boss into custody. Hopefully Ramer lives. He's the type to roll on his partner for a reduced sentence."

The last thing she wanted was Ramer waking up and giving a statement.

My God! Was she really wishing for a man to die?

"What happens if he doesn't?" she managed, her voice so low she barely heard herself.

"Well, if he doesn't make it, I guess you're in the clear. If he does, we'll have to get our stories straight."

She cocked her head. "What—what do you mean?"

"I kept your secret, Miss Whitman. I didn't mention Damien was even there, let alone what happened to him. But if Ramer wakes and tells a different story..."

"Won't people think he's crazy?"

He shrugged. "Probably. That's one of the reasons I didn't say anything."

"One of the reasons?"

"Yeah. Another was that, despite what you think of me, I

am a good guy. I don't understand what happened to Mr. Stone, but I know he was only protecting you. And that makes him okay in my book."

She threw her arms around him. "Thank you."

He awkwardly patted her back.

She pulled away. "I appreciate it. Truly."

"Mr. Stone." He scoffed and shook his head.

She joined him in a laugh. Mr. Stone, indeed.

A little over an hour later, a doctor came into the waiting room. "Detective? A word."

Urbani joined the doctor for a brief conversation. Try though she might, she couldn't overhear a word.

The doctor went back through the door, and Urbani returned to her. "It doesn't do anything for my case against my boss, but it helps you out. Ramer didn't make it."

She'd never been so conflicted. So relieved for Damien. Relieved for herself and Gretchen—Ramer couldn't chase them any longer. But rejoicing for a man's death? It was just so wrong.

Rina burst into tears.

Urbani embraced her, holding her until she'd settled down. Finally, she pulled away and mopped at the wet spots on his shirt. "I'm sorry."

"Don't worry about it."

"But it looks expensive." He always dressed well. She probably couldn't even afford to dry-clean the shirt, let alone replace it.

"Want to make it up to me?"

She blinked and looked up at him.

"Put a good word in for me to your friend."

"Gretchen?"

"Yeah. She's... spunky. I like that."

Rina smiled. "You've got yourself a deal."

Twenty-One

As usual, Damien spent the day yelling to Anael. And as usual, the angel remained silent. His body tingled. Probably less than an hour before he was released from his stone prison. Then he'd be free to—

To what? The list was long and varied. Check on Rina. Find and throttle that angel. Intimidate the detective into silence. Permanently silence Ramer.

Okay, it wasn't that varied. Most of it included violence.

"Damien."

The angel's voice in his head startled him. How he wished he could scream at him. Reach out and actually strangle the guy.

"No need for violence." Anael appeared beside him. "We need to talk. Can I trust that if I wake you before sunset, you'll behave, or should we continue in this manner?"

"You can wake me early?"

"Of course. I'm the one responsible for you being a gargoyle. Surely you realize I have the power to revive you at my whim."

Damien thought a slew of curses at him.

"Perhaps I'll leave you in this state for a bit."

Damien took a deep breath. At least, he paused and imagined breathing. Once he calmed, he thought to Anael. "I'm fine. I'll behave. Please, revive me."

"Hmm," the angel said. "Better safe than sorry."

Rage burbled inside him, but he settled when Anael raised his hand. Damien expected to be awakened, but instead, he was once again exploded into molecules, his cells scattering into the ether.

He reformed in an agonizing implosion in a meadow. At least he was in human form and was spared that transformation.

"How many times to I have to ask you not to do that?"

"I'm not sure you've ever asked me, Damien. You usually just demand I not do it."

"I do not."

Anael waved his hand. "Doesn't matter. Do you know where you are?"

He studied his surroundings. A "field" probably wasn't the answer Anael was going for.

The angel glared at him. "This is where you died. This very spot, in fact."

Damien stared at the ground beneath his feet then looked across the vast expanse of grasses. He didn't recognize the area, but it was dark out, and much had probably changed as the centuries passed. Besides, the last time he was there, the land was crowded with men and flooded with their blood.

"What are you thinking?" Anael asked.

"I thought you always knew what was in my head."

"At the moment, I prefer not exploring your thoughts. I'd rather you just tell me."

Damien thought nothing. Felt nothing. Finally, he said, "Over the years, I often reflected on the battle. I tried to remember every detail about this place. I have to admit, it's not what I expected."

"What did you expect?"

"I don't know. Not this. I guess I always see it in my head the way it was that day. The carnage. The devastation."

"And now?"

"Now it's just a meadow. Unimportant. Nondescript."

"What does that tell you?" Anael asked.

Damien stared across the great vista of indigenous flora, took in the twinkling fireflies and the scent of lavender blowing on the breeze. "It's peaceful here. Tranquil." He again conjured the memory of the battle and marveled that it was the same place. "Things change. Sometimes for the better."

"Not just things, Damien. Not just things."

"I get your point, Anael."

"Do you? Because it's time to make your decision. And the danger isn't over."

The danger? Could he still go to hell?

Fuck. He probably deserved to for even thinking about staying and ruining her life.

"I need to talk to Katarina."

"Of course."

Before Damien could prepare, his atoms were blown apart again.

Damien reassembled inside Rina's apartment, the implosion of molecules like fire through his veins. He panted, struggled for breath, and again cursed Anael in his thoughts.

"Damien?" Rina asked. "Are you all right?"

He bent and rested his elbows on his knees, took a few deep breaths. "Fine. Just... adjusting."

"Can I get you anything?"

"No, thanks. I'm good." He stood, stretched. Looked at her.

"Do you want to sit?" She nodded toward the sofa.

"I guess it's time we had that talk, huh?" He walked over to the sofa and sat.

She joined him, curled up in the corner.

"Seems I got us in a bit of a jam. At least, I got me into one."

"Us, Damien. We're in this together."

He shook his head. "See, that's the thing. You don't *have* to be part of this."

"I'm with you. No matter what. Besides, things aren't as bad as you think."

"Rina, one of the most important parts of my deal was not revealing myself to anyone. Not only did you find out before I'd earned back my humanity permanently, other people know now, too. Gretchen. Urbani. Ramer. Probably countless other innocents who might have been looking out their windows or passing by."

"First of all, you should tell your soul mate everything, including who you are. So, no, I don't think me learning is an issue. Second, Gretchen doesn't remember anything. Third, Ramer is dead."

Damien's head snapped up. "He... he didn't make it?"

She shook her head.

"So, I was brought back to learn the difference between killing for war and murdering for anger, and as soon as I figure it out, I kill someone."

"He was a bad man, Damien."

He hung his head in his hands.

"But you didn't kill him."

"I fell on him. In stone. Crushed him under me. I felt his bones snap, heard his moans. I may not have been animated, but I was alert."

"Then you should also have heard the gun fire. Because Detective Urbani shot him."

Damien stood and paced around her coffee table. "Does he know, too?"

"It's okay." She walked over to him, placed her hand on his arm. "He won't say anything."

"Sure."

"No, really. I've talked to him. He's already given his statement, and he didn't mention the transformation-thing. Didn't mention you at all, in fact, and he won't. Think about it... people would think he's crazy."

"Doesn't matter. I'm sure he still thinks I'm a monster. That I'm a threat to humanity. That I need to be put down."

"Actually, he told me he could tell you were a good man. See, Damien? You're safe. We can be together."

For the first time, he met her gaze, studied it. Read in her eyes unspoken hope and acceptance. Love. He wanted nothing more than to be the man she thought him to be. The man she deserved. Just before embracing it all, realization dawned.

He shook his head. "I don't know how to be the man you need. How to provide for you. How to fit into your world."

"What's your alternative? Eternity in hell? Don't be ridiculous."

He walked over to the window then looked down to the street. People bustled about, talking on phones, typing on them. Cars cruised back and forth, struggling to park or to navigate through pedestrians. One luxury black sedan squeezed into a space right in front of her building. A man in a trench coat got out then hurried inside. All that rushing. All that technology. He didn't understand it. Didn't know how to be a part of it.

"Katarina, I won't let you serve a sentence to spare me. I can't have you be with me because you don't want me to go to hell."

"Too bad. I can't have you go to hell because I want to be with you. It's not a hardship for me, Damien. I love you."

Love. She loved him? Was it possible? After all she'd seen him do? After considering all the ways he fell short?

"Did you hear me?" Her tone held tinges of uncertainty, desperation, and pain. "I love you."

He crossed to her, embraced her. Thrilled when she hugged him back. "I love you, too, Katarina. I have since the moment I saw you."

"So, what's the problem?" She pulled away and met his gaze.

"I don't understand this world."

"You'll learn. I'll help you."

"What will I do about a job? About a purpose in life?"

"Damien, you've been a warrior for centuries. You've helped people as a human and as a gargoyle. We'll ask Al to give you credentials to be a cop. Well, maybe that's too rigid. You could work security at the club. No, I want us out of there. Oh, I know. You can be a private investigator. I'll help you. I don't care what you do, as long as you do it here."

"Don't you have school to finish?"

"I'm a history major. What can I do with that degree? Nothing. But dealing with Ramer, watching you work to put him away—"

"That wasn't exactly what I was doing."

"You worked to keep me safe. That's exciting to me. I want to help people, too. I want to protect them. We'll do it together."

"You really think this can work?"

She smiled. "We love each other. The rest is just details. We'll figure it out."

Damien again reached for her, intent to embrace his soul mate as well as his destiny. Before he got to her, the door of her apartment flew open. The man from the street—the one wearing a trench coat and hurrying from the sedan—stepped inside and slammed the door behind him.

"You've been more damn trouble to me than any criminal I've ever dealt with in thirty-eight years on the force."

"Who are you?" Damien stepped in front of Rina, shielding her.

"Me? I'm the guy you have the whole fucking force looking for. Captain Renaldi. But you probably know me better as Dylan Ramer's connection."

Rina stepped out from behind Damien and approached the captain. "But, Detective Urbani said Internal Affairs was arresting you. He said we were safe."

"I have a whole network at my disposal. I knew IA was coming, and I got away. So, I'm here to tie up the loose ends Ramer left behind."

"But—"

Renaldi took his hand from his pocket. In it he held a gun. Pointed it right at Rina.

Damien stared in horror, petrified. Immovable, like stone. What was she doing?

His heart leapt into his throat. Finally, he jumped into action, but in his human form, he'd never be fast enough.

Renaldi fired.

Even if Damien hadn't frozen, he'd have been too late.

The bullet ripped through Rina's chest. She collapsed into Damien's arms. They both fell to the floor, where he rolled on top of her to protect her.

The captain continued to fire, the bullets ripping through her furniture, skimming just over top of Damien's head and back.

"Freeze!"

Damien couldn't see who spoke, so he looked up.

Detective Urbani stood in the doorway, gun trained on his former captain.

Renaldi turned, gun still raised.

Urbani fired.

Pink mist exploded from Renaldi's brain. He fell, lifeless, to the floor.

"Everyone okay?" Urbani asked.

Damien shook his head. "She needs help." He splayed his hand over the wound in her stomach, but the blood just oozed out from underneath his palm.

"I'll call it in."

Anael appeared. "That won't be necessary, Detective."

⁜

"Anael!" Damien yelled. "Do something!"

"That's why I'm here." He knelt beside Rina, placed his hand on her head, and closed his eyes. "She'll be dead in minutes. No doctor can save her now."

"But you can, right?"

The angel shook his head.

"Damn it, Anael! You said she was my destiny. You made me human for her!"

"No, Damien. I didn't make you human. You did that. You always had it in you. But you never found a reason to express that side of you until she came along."

"But now that I have a reason, now that my deal is done, you take her from me?"

"I'm not taking her. That's not my place. And I tried to warn you."

"When?"

"In the field, but you thought I meant hell, not gunfire."

"You bastard! You knew I didn't understand, but you let me come in here unprepared? I could kill you!" He lunged at the angel.

Anael just pushed him back. "No, you can't. More to the point, you shouldn't try. At least, not now. She only has seconds left, Damien. I suggest you spend them with her."

Damien dropped to his knees and took her hand. "I'm so sorry, Katarina. This is all my fault."

"Al," she whispered.

Damien sniffled. Tears fell from his eyes. "He's here. He'll take care of you. Take you straight to Heaven."

She shook her head. "Anael." Her voice was weak, faint.

"I'm here." The angel bent toward her, put his ear near her mouth.

She whispered something, but Damien couldn't hear her.

Anael sat up. His brow raised, and a smile crossed his face.

"What'd she say?" Damien asked.

Anael didn't answer.

Damien reanimated with a roar and a stretch. He climbed off his plinth, his claws scraping on the ashlar before he stepped onto the roof.

He really thought when he met Rina that his time as a gargoyle was over—hell or humanity, but never a grotesque again.

Never in his wildest dreams did he expect to agree to spend an eternity as one.

He unfurled his wings and looked to the plinth next to his.

A female gargoyle also stretched her wings. She looked at him and smiled.

"Have a nice rest?" he asked.

"I did. Wish I had been cuddling you, though."

He laughed. "I think the people below would have noticed that."

Rina smiled. "Probably. But they can't see us now. Race you?"

"You're feisty tonight."

"I want to visit the catfish. Then we'll take human form and look for people to help. Urbani might have something for us. Someone we can help that he can't."

"Or we could grab a sandwich and a beer. Visit Gretchen and Tiny."

"We can do it all." She smiled again. "We have all night."

"We have forever." Damien grabbed her hand then pulled her toward him. He kissed the ridges on her head, rubbed her horns. "I can't believe you did this for me."

"I didn't. I did it for us." She took off, soaring into the cloud bank.

Damien crouched then sprang up after her. Only one thing beat the feeling of gliding through the skies, having a close-up view of the stars and moon.

It was doing it with the woman he loved.

Her laughter carried to him on the breeze, and he pushed harder to catch up to her. Damien never wanted to be without Katarina again. Thanks to Anael, he never had to be.

Thank You

Ciao, amici!

Thank you for taking the time to read *Love Set in Stone*. If you enjoyed it, please consider telling your friends and posting a short review. Word of mouth is an author's best friend, helps more than you could possibly know, and is much appreciated.

Staci

Also by Staci Troilo

SERIES

Cathedral Lake Series

Type and Cross (Book 1)

Out and About (Book 2)

Pride and Fall (Book 3)

Footprints in the Snow (Short Story to be Read after Book 1)

Medici Protectorate Series

Bleeding Heart (Book 1)

Mind Control (Book 2)

Body Armor (Book 3)

Tortured Soul (Book 4)

Valuable Treasures (Prequel Short Story)

Keystone Couples Series

No Such Luck (Novella 1)

Pour it On (Novella 2)

Between the Vines (Novella 3)

STAND ALONE NOVELS

The Haunting of Chatham Hollow (co-authored)

Mystery Heir

NOVELLAS

A Fathomless Affair
When We Finally Kiss Goodnight
Laci and Del: 12 Months, 12 Chances

ANTHOLOGIES

Unshod (Warrior of Blanca Peak)
Macabre Sanctuary (The All Souls Ritual)
Quantum Wanderlust (Vicious Circle)
Bright Lights and Candle Glow (The No in Noel)

About the Author

Staci Troilo grew up in a family-focused home. In addition to spending so much quality time with her parents and siblings, she was blessed to visit with grandparents, aunts, uncles, and/or cousins daily, not just on holidays or weekends. Because of those close-knit bonds, every day was full of love and laughter, food and fun.

Life took her away from that extended family, and while she does her best to keep traditions alive across the miles, she knows there truly is no place like home.

Through her fiction, she shares her traditions and her conviction that close relationships are of the utmost importance. Mystery or suspense, romance or mainstream, sci-fi or thriller—in her stories, family (however you define it) is paramount.

stacitroilo.com

www.ingramcontent.com/pod-product-compliance
Lightning Source LLC
Chambersburg PA
CBHW071306250626
47159CB00004B/1326